Birthday

A Rainey Daye Cozy Mystery, book 5

by

Kathleen Suzette

Books by Kathleen Suzette:
A Rainey Daye Cozy Mystery Series

Clam Chowder and a Murder
A Rainey Daye Cozy Mystery, book 1
A Short Stack and a Murder
A Rainey Daye Cozy Mystery, book 2
Cherry Pie and a Murder
A Rainey Daye Cozy Mystery, book 3
Barbecue and a Murder
A Rainey Daye Cozy Mystery, book 4
Birthday Cake and a Murder
A Rainey Daye Cozy Mystery, book 5
Hot Cider and a Murder
A Rainey Daye Cozy Mystery, book 6
Roast Turkey and a Murder
A Rainey Daye Cozy Mystery, book 7
Gingerbread and a Murder
A Rainey Daye Cozy Mystery, book 8
Fish Fry and a Murder
A Rainey Daye Cozy Mystery, book 9
Cupcakes and a Murder
A Rainey Daye Cozy Mystery, book 10
Lemon Pie and a Murder
A Rainey Daye Cozy Mystery, book 11
Pasta and a Murder
A Rainey Daye Cozy Mystery, book 12
Chocolate Cake and a Murder
A Rainey Daye Cozy Mystery, book 13

A Pumpkin Hollow Mystery Series

Candy Coated Murder
A Pumpkin Hollow Mystery, book 1
Murderously Sweet
A Pumpkin Hollow Mystery, book 2
Chocolate Covered Murder

A Gracie Williams Mystery Series

Pushing Up Daisies in Arizona,
A Gracie Williams Mystery, Book 1
Kicked the Bucket in Arizona,
A Gracie Williams Mystery, Book 2

A Home Economics Mystery Series

Appliqued to Death
A Home Economics Mystery, book 1

Table of Contents

Chapter One

"CAN'T YOU STOP THAT racket? This is a civilized neighborhood!"

I stared bleary-eyed at the elderly man standing on my doorstep. "I'm sorry. I know she's loud, but she doesn't mean any harm. I'll take care of it." I could hear my dog, Maggie, barking incessantly at something in my backyard. Maggie was a Bluetick Coonhound, so to say she was barking was an understatement. She was in full hound dog bay-mode. I glanced at the clock leaning against the overstuffed armchair three feet from me. 7:16.

The man squinted his eyes at me, peering at the cardboard boxes behind me, his red-and-blue plaid shirt unbuttoned to reveal a dingy white T-shirt. "Land sakes, I don't know what this neighborhood is coming to. You aren't moving in here, are you?"

I stared at him, still groggy with sleep. Hadn't he seen the U-Haul truck parked in the driveway most of the previous day? "Yes, I am moving in here. I bought this house." He had a head full of white hair that stuck up in places, and he was unshaven, his beard-stubble matching the hair on his head.

He snorted and looked me up and down. I thought he must be in his early seventies and he was none too pleased to meet me. "It seems like you could cover up before opening the door. This is a decent neighborhood."

I pulled my pink bathrobe tighter around me, and he gave me one more disapproving look before turning and heading to the house next door. I glanced down at myself. I was wearing a T-shirt and shorts beneath the robe. If he considered that revealing, he had a funny idea of revealing.

I shut the door and turned and headed to the back door. The cute little cottage I had seen a couple of months earlier was finally all mine, with a lot of financial help from my mother. I was surprised she had volunteered so readily, but I was grateful. It was everything I had ever wanted in a house.

I unlocked the back door that was off the kitchen and looked out into the yard. The summer heat hadn't been kind to the lawn, but I would figure out how to care for it. I figured I'd have it green as could be by next spring. The previous day's downpour of rain had broken a long dry spell and had made moving challenging and messy.

"Maggie!" I called from the cement patio. I had rescued Maggie from the county shelter a couple of months earlier after she had helped save me from a murderer. After what we had been through together, there was no way I was leaving her behind. "Maggie!"

Maggie was digging at the ground along the back fence, and I figured she must have sniffed out a rabbit or squirrel on the other side.

"Maggie, come here!" I called. She stopped her barking and looked over her shoulder, then went back to barking and digging, a whine escaping between barks now and then. Whatever was on the other side of the fence was tormenting her.

"Quiet that dog down!" I heard my new neighbor yell from an open window next door.

I sighed. There's nothing like getting off on the wrong foot with the new neighbors.

"Maggie!" She turned and trotted over to me, her tail wagging. Mud ran up her front legs as high as her elbows, and a clump of mud clung to the end of her black nose.

"You have to hush," I whispered, bending over and rubbing her head. "We have hostile neighbors. Let's get some breakfast." I turned to head back inside, and she turned in the opposite direction and went back to where she had been digging in the mud.

"Maggie, please," I said under my breath and went after her. I stopped when my slipper-clad feet sank into the mud. The white bunny slippers I was so fond of soaked up the water and mud, and my feet were suddenly wet. I slipped them off and went to Maggie, taking her by the collar and leading her toward the house. "Come on, Maggie, let's be nice on our first day in our new house."

She whined in protest but complied with my wishes.

Inside the house, I poured kibble into her bowl and went to the coffeemaker to get the coffee started. I was going to need it. I was exhausted. My identical twin sister Stormy, my mother, and my boyfriend, Detective Cade Starkey, had spent the day before packing and moving. I didn't have a lot of furniture, so my mother gave me some of hers. She had wanted to buy new furniture anyway, and I was thrilled. It was one less expense for me.

Maggie inhaled her breakfast and then was at the back door, scratching to be let out. I sighed. "Listen, Maggie. I know you're technically a hunting dog and I'm sure there's some tasty varmint on the other side of the fence, but the thing is, we apparently have a grumpy neighbor and all that barking is going to get me into trouble."

She whined in response, her forehead wrinkling.

"You're not going out," I said firmly and went to my bedroom to clean off the mud from my feet and get dressed while the coffee percolated. I would save cleaning up Maggie and the mess she had made on my kitchen floor for later.

I rinsed my feet in the bathtub, grabbed a clean T-shirt and jeans, and got dressed. I had so many plans for my new house. It was adorable with its vintage accents in most of the rooms and a full-sized basement that I would eventually have made into a second bathroom and two additional bedrooms. That would come later, of course. Funds were currently in short supply. I had lost my job in New York City and now worked part-time at Sam's Diner while I worked on an Americana-themed cookbook. Without my mother's financial help, I would never have been able to buy this house. I hated owing her though, so I was working on ways to bring in more money.

I heard my phone go off, and I grabbed it from the straight-backed chair next to my bed. I would have to buy end tables at some point. There was a text from my sister.

Good morning, Sis! Hope you slept well.

I snorted. While it was touching that she was thinking of me, she had left my house at nearly midnight, and I had stayed up another two hours unpacking. I was beat, and I figured she was too. Unpacking could have waited, but I was so excited about the new house that I couldn't sleep.

I slept ok, I guess. My charming neighbor pounded on the door complaining about Maggie's barking first thing this morning.

Aw, sad face. I'd pick up breakfast for you, but I've got to get the kids to school.

My sister had five kids, the oldest of which had gone off to college in California the previous weekend. Stormy was emotional about the whole thing, and I made a mental note to take her out to lunch soon and cheer her up.

I could hear Maggie scratching at the kitchen door and becoming more frantic. I sighed, setting my phone back on the chair, and headed back to do damage control.

"Seriously, Maggs?" I said. I reached for the doorknob to go out and see what had her so interested, then thought better of it. She'd make a mad dash for the great outdoors and start barking again. I already had one mark against me where that neighbor was concerned, and I wondered if the neighbor on the other side of me was grumpy too.

I put a leash on Maggie and tied her to the knob on the front door, then headed back to the kitchen. The patio was covered and had provided some protection from the rain, but the yard itself was flooded. My shoes sank into the wet ground as I crossed the yard.

The fence was solid wood, six feet tall, and painted white. The tops of the boards were cut at an angle. It felt very 1950s-ish and something about it made me happy when I looked at it.

I saw the metal latch on the gate and reminded myself to get a padlock for it. Sparrow, Idaho, was a small town, and while we didn't have the crime that larger cities did, it paid to be safe.

The gate creaked as I pushed it open and peered around it. The city hadn't gotten around to paving the alleys on this side of town, and the rain had made it a muddy mess. I wished I had put rain boots on before coming outside.

The house was in an older part of town where the houses were built between the early 1940s to late 1950s. I stepped into a deep mud puddle and winced as my gray tennis shoes sank into it. The big green dumpsters in the alley were shared between neighbors, and I wondered if a cat was digging in the open trash bin that was nearest my fence. I thought the trash people were going to be unhappy when trying to dump that thing. The downpour we'd had must have filled it up at least halfway.

I waded carefully through the mud, my arms outstretched like a windmill, toward the dumpster. I slipped twice before I got to it, but thanks to my windmill skills, I managed to remain on my feet. There was a blue tarp on the ground on the far side of the dumpster, and I made my way around, thinking a small animal may have found refuge from the storm beneath it. When a gust blew across the alley, the corner of the tarp flew up in the air and flapped in the breeze. My breath caught in my throat when I saw a hand lying motionless beneath the tarp.

Chapter Two

I BIT MY LOWER LIP to keep from screaming, and stared at the hand sticking out from beneath the tarp. When the breeze died down, the flap lay almost completely over the hand, covering it. Part of my mind refused to believe what I had just seen, but it was too early for Halloween, so I knew it wasn't part of someone's display or costume.

Against my better judgment, I moved in closer and tucked the toe of my shoe beneath the edge of the tarp and lifted it a bit. There was more than a hand beneath it. There was a whole body. Whoever put this person out here had tucked the edges of the tarp beneath the body to keep it from flying away in the breeze.

I felt my front jeans pockets for my phone and realized it wasn't there, so I ran back into the house for it. Maggie whined when I ran past her to get my phone.

The phone was on the chair in my bedroom and I grabbed it and dialed Cade's number, doing a nervous little dance while waiting for him to pick up. Maggie whined for me from the living room.

"Hello, Gorgeous," Cade said brightly. "You're up early."

"Cade, there's a body in my alley," I said, trying to catch my breath.

"A what in your what?" he asked.

"A body. A dead body. In my alley. The alley behind my house," I explained between gulping breaths.

There was a pause.

"Are you serious?" he finally asked.

"Why would I kid about something like that?" I asked him. "You need to come here and do something with it."

"I just stepped out of the shower and I need to get dressed. You stay put and I'll be there in a few minutes."

I nodded and realized he couldn't see that. "Okay, but hurry," I said.

"I will. And Rainey?"

"Yes?" I said, still breathing hard.

"Don't mess with the crime scene," he said.

I sighed and rolled my eyes. "I wouldn't do something like that!"

"Sure you wouldn't, but I'm serious. I'll be right there." The phone went dead.

Having a dead body right outside my house creeped me out. I went back into the living room, pacing back and forth, and then I realized that one of the neighbors might run into the body out there. I didn't want someone to have to see that, and I didn't want someone trudging through the crime scene. As much as I hated the thought, I knew I needed to go back out there. Taking Maggie with me would make me feel safer, but I knew she would try to get to the body to check it out.

"I'll be back soon, Maggie," I said and went back outside. I hadn't stopped to scrape off the excess mud from my shoes before running into the house to find my phone and I had made a mess of my floors. I would deal with that later.

The body was where I had left it and the neighborhood was quiet. It was still early for some people to be out and about while others had already left for work. There were wide tire tracks in the mud near the body and I wondered if it was from someone dumping trash in the dumpsters or if it was from the killer's vehicle.

In spite of Cade's warning, I tiptoed closer to the body, keeping an eye on the mud to make sure I didn't disturb anything that could be evidence. The body was lying face up, judging by the position of the hand. The flap of tarp blew up again, and I saw it was the person's left hand, palm up. There was no wedding ring on it and it was large enough to be a man's hand. I lifted the edge of the tarp with my shoe again. I didn't want to see, but I had to. I wasn't sure if I could live with my decision if it was someone I knew well, or if there was severe trauma to the body, but I needed to know if I knew who this was.

The tarp was firmly tucked beneath the body and all I could see was a man's chambray blue work shirt-clad arm. I would have to untuck the tarp from beneath his torso if I was going to get a better look. I considered going straight to where his head would be to see if I recognized who this was, but decided against it and let the tarp fall back. I didn't want to discover a nasty surprise. Cade would be furious if he knew I was messing with the body, so it might not have been a great idea, but I needed to know.

I made my way around the body, looking for another entry point and loosened the tarp at the other end to reveal a brown suede boot, similar to the kind people wore when hiking in the woods. There wasn't any mud in the waffle soles and I figured he must have been killed prior to it raining, or killed somewhere else.

My eyes traveled along the ground, hoping to find something else that would help explain what had happened here. Something sticking out of the mud near the tire tracks glinted in the sun. I carefully made my way over to it, and then squatted down. It was a silver ballpoint pen. There was printing on the barrel and I glanced over my shoulder to make sure Cade wasn't nearby before wiping some of the mud from it with the hem of my shirt. Squinting, I strained to read the green lettering.

Sparrow Daily News

There was an address and phone number beneath the name. We only had one newspaper in town and they published a ten-sheet paper every weekday evening. There was never much in there, just the local happenings, obituaries, and advertisements for local businesses. I left the pen where it was and stood up and looked over at the tarp again. The pen may have been trash or it may have belonged to whoever was under the tarp.

I carefully headed back to the tarp and went over who I might know that worked at the newspaper. Richard Price. He was Stormy's husband's cousin and worked on typesetting the newspaper. Sparrow's only paper had never had enough money to come into the digital age and was printed on old typesetting machinery from the 1960s. I hoped it wasn't him.

I carefully stepped back from the tarp and looked at the mud. There were a lot of footprints in the area, including mine. I started carefully walking backward, trying to step in the prints I had already made. Cade would notice. Nothing escaped him.

The tire tracks by themselves weren't suspicious since someone may have driven back here to dump trash and there were so many footprints it would make things hard to figure out which, if any, belonged to the killer.

I made my way over to the open dumpster and looked over the side. As expected, it was nearly half-full of water. Assorted garbage floated on the surface while white and black plastic trash bags filled the bottom. The bin had only been slightly over the half-full mark when it began raining. I didn't see anything suspicious at first, but then I spotted what looked like a dark raincoat near a black trash bag. I couldn't be certain it was a raincoat without pulling it out of the bin though, so I stood on tiptoe and reached for it. My fingers just grazed it, but I wasn't tall enough and couldn't get a hold on it. The bin stank and flies hovered in the morning sunlight. I took a step back.

I pulled my phone from my pocket. It had been about ten minutes since I had called Cade and he said he needed to get dressed. If I knew him, he would be here any minute now. I carefully made my way back to the gate to wait.

It was less than a minute when Cade slowly drove down the alley. He parked near where I stood and got out of his car, his hair still wet from his shower, and neatly slicked back.

"This is quite a welcome to the neighborhood," he said, giving me a quick kiss. He smelled like aftershave and toothpaste.

"One I could have done without," I said.

"Tell me you haven't been snooping around the crime scene."

I looked at him. "There have been any number of people back here in the alley recently." I forced myself not to look at my footprints in the mud.

He sighed. "I hope you didn't contaminate the crime scene."

"I didn't. I simply took a look in the dumpster and at those tire tracks over there." I pointed out the wide tire tracks.

His eyes went to my shoes, and he sighed.

Chapter Three

"DON'T SIGH AT ME," I said, folding my arms across my chest. "It's not like I knew there was a body under that tarp. Maggie was barking her head off and one of my new neighbors woke me up to complain. I came out to see what Maggie was barking at, and it never occurred to me that there was a body out here."

He ignored me and turned back to the tarp, squinting his eyes. "A body under the tarp," he muttered and looked at the ground in front of the tarp. "The things you find in an alley."

"Those are my footprints," I said, coming to stand beside him and pointing at the tracks I had made. "Just so you know."

"I see. You ignored what I said about contaminating the crime scene. Stay here," he said and carefully picked his way through the mud to the tarp. Cade and I hadn't been dating long. I had made his acquaintance when he took an interest in me on another murder case. An interest in me being a possible suspect, not a possible girlfriend.

I followed after him because I'm not very good at taking direction. "I did not contaminate the crime scene. And, it's a man under there. At least, I'm pretty sure it is, but I didn't pull the tarp all the way back."

He stopped and looked over his shoulder. "You didn't pull it all the way back? But you did pull it back some? Didn't I tell you not to mess with the crime scene?"

"I guess I forgot," I said, not looking him in the eye. "And besides, it's not like I was really messing with it. I just took a little look."

He snorted and turned back to the tarp, squatted down, and looked back up at me. "Turn away. You don't want to see this. And go back and stand by the gate."

I complied with him as far as turning away. "Is it someone we know?" I asked him. I heard the tarp rustle and I had to force myself not to look.

"It's not someone I know. Older guy. Early sixties, maybe."

I turned to look. I couldn't help myself, it was like a reflex. "Oh. That's Silas Mills. I think. He works at the newspaper." I wasn't completely sure because his skin was pasty looking. Silas had never looked very good, being extremely thin and anemic looking, but he really wasn't looking his best right now. Without a mortician to make dead people look good, it's a shock. At least it wasn't Richard Price, my brother-in-law's cousin.

"I told you not to look," Cade said and pulled the tarp back further.

I looked away again. Something had killed Silas, and I didn't want to see what that something was in case it was really bad. "How did he die?"

"Judging by the knife in his chest, I'd say by being stabbed. How well did you know Silas?"

"Not well. He was a fixture around town though. He covered local sports and I think I've occasionally seen his byline on other articles."

Cade sighed and pulled a camera out of his coat pocket. "I need you to go back and stand by your gate, please. I hope we haven't lost any evidence with you walking back and forth through here."

I frowned. "I'm sorry. I just didn't know there was a body under the tarp to begin with. I tried to backtrack over my footprints when I realized it was there. And there's a pen from the newspaper stuck in the mud over there."

"Got it. Please go stand by the gate," he said, laying the tarp back over Silas's body. Cade pulled his phone from his pocket and made a phone call asking for the coroner.

I turned and headed back, leaning against the fence. He took pictures of the ground around the body, including the tire tracks, footprints, and the pen. "Do you know Silas's next of kin?" he asked.

"I'm not sure if I do. I don't remember hearing if he was married or not," I said as he continued taking pictures.

"What kind of articles besides sports did he write for the newspaper?" he asked.

Cade had only lived in Sparrow for a few months and didn't know many people yet. Sometimes it took a while to acclimate in small towns. People were friendly, but trust could be a whole different issue. Especially since he was law enforcement.

I thought back. "I think he covered the Christmas parade last December. And there was a rodeo in April. I can't really remember anything big."

"I can't see how writing an article on the Christmas parade would make someone mad enough to kill him," he said, grinning at me.

"I don't know. Things can get volatile when Santa doesn't throw enough candy to the kids during the parade."

He chuckled. "I guess I can see where things might get testy in that case."

"You have no idea. I once saw the Marston triplets and the Green twins in a throw down for the last candy cane. You should have seen those kids go at it. Then their parents jumped right in the middle of it. Santa had no remorse for his actions. I'm pretty sure he was chuckling behind that white beard of his."

"You gotta keep your eye on Santa," he said and headed toward me as we heard sirens in the distance.

"Why the sirens? He's already dead," I said.

He shrugged. "Some people are just zealous about their jobs. What else do you know about Silas?"

I thought about it. What had I heard? I didn't know him well, but occasionally he came into the diner. I had put an ad in the paper last month when my mother wanted to have a yard sale and he had been sitting at one of the desks. I knew him enough to say hello, but I really didn't know him well at all.

"If I remember right, he lives, or lived, down at the Sparrow Boardinghouse."

"Boardinghouse? Do those things even exist anymore?" he asked me.

"They do in sparrow. It's across town and not in a very good area. It seems like a lot of older people live there, and maybe other people that don't have family."

"Is it like a real boardinghouse? Rooms can be rented on a week-to-week basis? And is there a woman that owns it and does she make meals where everyone eats together?"

I chuckled. "Are you sure you haven't been there? That's pretty much the way it's run by Sue Hester, the woman that owns it. Although I do think she's getting up there in years. I have to wonder how much longer it will be around."

"Running a boardinghouse is a lost art."

"Do you think he was dumped here? Could he have been killed here in the alley?" I asked as a squad car pulled up, parking behind Cade's car.

"I doubt he was killed here in the alley. The killer would have had to just happen to have that tarp with them and would have to lure him out here. I would bet that whoever killed him had some feelings for him."

"Why do you say that?" I asked, looking at the blue tarp.

"They were careful to tuck the tarp under his body as if to shield him from the weather. If they didn't feel something for him, they wouldn't have cared if he was out here in the rain."

I nodded. "I guess that makes sense. I wonder why he's here if he lived across town," I said.

"That's a good question. One we'll have to try to figure out," he said and turned to the officer that approached us and began filling him in on what he knew so far.

The two of them stepped away from me to go over the details. I wondered how Silas Mills had ended up dead in the alley behind my house and I hoped what Cade said was true. If the killer cared for Silas that meant it was personal and they probably wouldn't be out killing random people. In the meantime, I was going to make sure all the locks on my windows and doors were in working order.

Chapter Four

"I BROUGHT YOU A HOUSEWARMING gift!" my mother said excitedly. She stood on my front porch and in her arms was a two-feet tall ficus tree with a big pink ribbon tied around the white faux marble pot it was in. Stormy was standing behind her with a gift bag in her hand.

"Wow, that's so sweet of you, Mom," I said and stepped aside for them to enter.,

"You need something to brighten the room and a plant always does that," she said, looking around at the cardboard boxes on the floor in the living room. "What have you been doing all day? Why isn't the furniture arranged, and the boxes unpacked?"

"How are you doing, Stormy?" I asked, ignoring my mother. Stormy had sad eyes as she handed me the gift bag. I knew her oldest daughter's departure was the cause of her sadness. She had been struggling for months with the fact that it was going to happen, and now it had.

"I'm fine. I got you a little something for the kitchen," she said and looked around. "We can help you unpack if you want."

"I don't want to unpack, I've worked all day. What's for dinner?" Mom asked, heading to the kitchen doorway.

"Bad news. I've been kind of preoccupied today and didn't have time to go shopping for food. We'll order pizza."

"What? Seriously?" Mom asked, turning back to me. "I was looking forward to a meal cooked and served by my daughter, the famous cookbook author."

"Well, your not-so-famous daughter was otherwise tied up today. That's why everything's all over the house," I said, sitting on the loveseat in the middle of the room. I opened the gift bag Stormy had brought. "Oh, how cool!" I exclaimed as I pulled out a cute ceramic measuring cup set in the shape of a Bluetick hound dog's head. "Where did you find these?"

"It was a search, let me tell you, but the Internet never lets me down," she said, smiling. "I'm sure you have more than your fair share of measuring cups, but I couldn't resist."

"I can always use measuring cups and these are darling. Thank you! And thank you, Mom, for the ficus tree. You're right, it will brighten things up."

"A proper thank you would be a home-cooked meal," Mom groused, sitting on an over-stuffed chair sitting off to the side of the room.

I ignored her. Mom wasn't being cranky, that was just how she was.

"Stormy, how is Natalie doing at college?" I asked as I took the measuring cups into the kitchen and then returned to the loveseat.

She shrugged. "I guess she's doing okay. She's homesick. I told her she could transfer back to Idaho State next semester."

"I bet she'll adjust. Natalie is a resourceful girl," I assured her.

"She's only seventeen," Stormy said with a whine in her voice. Stormy had been a child bride and a child mother, barely turning eighteen two months before Natalie was born. I thought she was crazy at the time, but she and Bob had been happily married for years.

"She'll be eighteen in less than three months. She's mature and ready for this. And even though you don't feel like it, so are you. The ready part, I mean."

Tears sprang to her eyes, and she nodded.

"Speaking of birthdays, the two of you have one coming up in a couple of weeks. Do either of you want anything special?" Mom asked.

"I want Natalie home," Stormy whimpered.

"You're not getting it. She's grown up now. What else do you want?" Mom said.

"You've done enough for me by helping me buy this house," I told her. "You don't need to get me anything else."

"Well, I'm starving. Let's order pizza. We can help unpack while we wait for it to be delivered," Mom said, getting to her feet.

"You got it," I said and pulled out my phone and placed the order.

"So what had you tied up all day?" Mom asked as she took a box labeled 'kitchen' into the kitchen to unpack.

Stormy and I picked up boxes that belonged in the kitchen and followed after her. "Silas Mills was killed and someone dumped his body in my alley."

"What?" Mom and Stormy said together.

I nodded, putting the box on the old table that had been discarded by one of Mom's neighbors. It was a little rickety and scuffed, but it would work for now. "Yeah. Maggie was barking her head off this morning, and a neighbor came to complain. Silas was out under a tarp in the alley." I filled them in on what little I knew so far. Cade had spent the better part of the day out there until the coroner came and picked up the body.

"How sad," Stormy said. "And you never heard a thing?"

"Not until my neighbor pounded on the door and woke me up. I was tired after moving yesterday, and I guess I was sleeping pretty hard."

"Sad indeed. Old Silas was at the newspaper for forever. I doubt he ever had any other job," Mom said as she unpacked a set of mixing bowls.

"Do you remember what kind of articles he wrote for the paper? I know he covered local sports at the schools, but I think I've seen other articles with his byline," I said and used a kitchen knife to cut through the tape holding my box closed.

"I think it was whatever needed writing," Mom said. "Oh, I do remember he wrote an article a few years back when Charlie Rhoades was running for city council. There was a big stink over it. Silas said Charlie Rhoades had spent time in jail years ago and wouldn't make a good city councilman."

"Really? So did he lose the election?" I asked.

She clucked her tongue. "Sure did. But the stink was mostly about the fact that Charlie Rhoades is Silas's cousin and the article caused a big rift in the family."

"Well that took some guts to write an expose' article on your own cousin," I said. It would also be a motive for murder, I thought.

"Makes you wonder if Charlie had anything to do with Silas's murder," Stormy said, reading my mind.

"Doesn't it though?" Mom said. "To make matters worse, last year Charlie moved into the boardinghouse where Silas lives."

"That's kind of crazy," I said. "I mean, he had to have known Silas was already living there. He's been there for years, hasn't he?"

"As long as I can remember," Mom said. "I can imagine those two living under the same roof. Things had to have been tense."

"Was Silas married?" I asked.

"No, he wasn't. I don't know if he ever did get married," Mom said.

"I think he was dating Karen Forrest. She works at the newspaper, too," Stormy added, coming over to help me unload the box I had on the table.

"What does she do there?" I asked. Karen lived two doors down from my mother and she would occasionally stop by to drop off a casserole or something she had made. I hadn't realized she was dating Silas.

"I think she writes lifestyle articles. Not that they publish much of those. Maybe she does something else, too," Mom said.

"Seems like they dated a long time," Stormy added.

"I think it has been a long time. Poor thing. She'll be destroyed over this," Mom said. "You should make her a cake and take it over. And make your mother one, too. I haven't had any of your cooking in forever."

I eyed her. "Mom, I made dinner for you two nights ago," I pointed out. "But I think making Karen a cake is a great idea. I feel bad that she lost someone she cared for." As soon as I said it, I remembered what Cade had said about the killer most likely being someone that cared about Silas. I needed to find out how much she did care.

"I like cake," Stormy said with a grin.

"So, I need to make three cakes?" I asked, pulling out the dishes from the box I was working on. "I need to wash all these dishes, they've been in storage for a while." I had lived with my mother ever since I moved back to Sparrow after my divorce, and nearly everything I owned had been in storage.

"You need a dishwasher," Mom said. "And you can make my cake smaller. Now that you've abandoned me, I'm all alone and I don't need a big cake."

I rolled my eyes at her. "If you hadn't helped me out with the house, I wouldn't have abandoned you."

"I need a big cake," Stormy said. "Five kids. Oh. No. Four kids." There was sadness in her voice when she said the last part.

I looked at her as tears sprang to her eyes and she blinked them back. "The holidays will be here before you know it and Natalie will be back for a visit. It will go fast. I promise."

"But what if she decides she wants to stay in California for the holidays?" she whined.

"Stop that. She will be here," I assured her.

"Rainey, you need to figure out what kind of cake you girls want for your birthday. And then make it. We'll have a party and you can invite Cade. He's family now, after all."

I shook my head and didn't say anything. Ever since Cade had come to town, Mom had been determined to get the two of us together and now that we were dating, she was going to try and get us married. It was far too early to think about that.

"I'll make the cake," I promised.

And I would speak to Karen and see if she knew anything about Silas Mills' murder.

Chapter Five

BEFORE I WENT INTO work at the diner the next day, I stopped off at Karen Forrest's house. I picked up Stormy on the way and with fall just around the corner, I made an apple crumb cake to take to Karen. Karen's car was parked out front and the shades were all pulled at her house when we got there.

I knocked at the door and heard footsteps on the other side. "Good morning, Karen," I said when she opened the door. Her eyes were red and puffy with dark circles beneath them. "I hope we're not disturbing you, but we wanted to stop by and say how sorry we were to hear about Silas."

"Good morning, Rainey, Stormy," she said. There was a tremble in her voice and she swallowed. "That's kind of you. Would you like to come in?"

She led us to the living room and offered us a seat on the couch. "I made you an apple crumb cake," I said, offering it to her.

She gave me a small smile. "That's sweet of you Rainey, you make the best food. Doesn't matter what it is, it's always great." She took the cake from me. "I do appreciate this."

"You're so welcome. I wish it were more. If there's anything we can do for you, don't hesitate to let us know."

"That's so nice of you. I'll just take this into the kitchen. Can I get you two some coffee?"

"No, thanks. I think I'm at capacity," Stormy said. I seconded that, and we waited in silence until she got back from putting the cake into the kitchen. The living room was bland with shades of beige and brown but was neatly kept.

Karen was in her late forties and often wore her medium brown hair in a bun at the back of her head. She seemed sweet and kept to herself, so much so that I wasn't even aware she had been dating Silas.

When she came back into the living room, she stopped and put her hands on her hips. She was a small woman, not much over five feet tall. "I'll tell you both something, I don't know what I'm going to do without Silas," she said with a hitch in her voice. "It just doesn't seem right."

"I can't imagine how hard this must be," I said. "Were you and Silas together long?"

She nodded and sat across from me. "Twenty years."

I tried to keep the surprise off my face. I had no idea they were even a couple. "Really? Twenty years?"

She smiled. "I know. We weren't much for bragging, but we just celebrated our twentieth anniversary."

"And you didn't want to get married?" It was out of my mouth before I realized she might consider it rude.

"I did. In the beginning, anyway. But Silas, he said he wasn't the marrying kind. Whatever that meant." She chuckled. "He never could explain that one to me. After a while, you just get used to being together and don't think about marriage."

"Some people are more comfortable that way," Stormy added.

I nodded, but I felt sorry for her. Twenty years was a long time to be with someone who wouldn't commit. It had to have worn on her and I wondered if it was a source of stress between them.

"I think that must have been hard. I guess if it was me, I would have insisted on marriage or moved on." It might not have been the kindest thing to say just then, but I wondered how much it bothered her for him to resist marriage.

She looked at me and blinked, considering this. "I guess I could have. And maybe I should have. But I didn't have the heart to do it. Besides, we were happy. We did the things we wanted to do. Silas could be charming when he wanted to be. And then, sometimes not so charming." She chuckled again, but it sounded weak and self-conscious.

"We all have our good days and our not so good days," I said, but I wondered what she meant by Silas having not so charming days.

"Sometimes when you're with someone a long time, you let your hair down," Stormy agreed. "Bob and I have been together since we were kids and some days it takes a lot of effort for me to be charming to him."

Karen smiled at Stormy. "That's certainly true, but I'll tell you girls, I just don't know who could have killed Silas. But then again, I suppose I could take a wild guess at it."

"Oh? Who do you think might want to kill Silas?" I asked.

She was quiet a moment and then turned to me. "I hate to point fingers, I really do. But, if I had to say who it might be, I would say it was Sue Hester at the boardinghouse." Her face pinched up when she said it and I thought she would start to cry, but she got herself under control.

"Why do you think it might be Sue?" I asked.

She shrugged. "I don't know. Maybe I shouldn't say it. But Sue had a thing for Silas. She's older than he is and he never did care for her. He said she kept pestering him to take her out to dinner and when he would refuse, he said she got angry."

"Did she know you were seeing Silas?"

"Of course. I went down to the boardinghouse quite a lot. I don't know why she had such an interest in him, but she sure did. She'd make eyes at him all the time, and then she'd be cold toward me."

"So do you think it was a case of unrequited love?" Stormy asked.

She shrugged. "That, or I'm just grief-stricken and trying to find someone to blame." She sat back in her chair and sighed.

"That's certainly understandable," I said. "Death is something that takes time to accept, much less understand."

She was quiet a moment. "I do know something about Sue, though," she said quietly.

"What's that?" I asked.

"She has a prison record."

That surprised me as much as Karen saying she and Silas had dated for twenty years. Sue must have been around seventy and she didn't appear to be someone that had lived a hardened life.

"What was she in prison for?" I asked.

"I don't know exactly. Silas told me about it one day. He said she spent her early twenties in the state penitentiary."

"How did Silas know and why didn't he tell you what she was in there for?" I asked. It seemed like if Silas knew Sue was in prison, then he would have told Karen the reason.

"He said she told him one day. He thought she wanted him to feel sorry for her and then maybe it would make him want to take her out on a date. Silas said there was no reason to spread it around if she didn't want anyone to know."

I considered this. "Except he did tell you."

She nodded. "He was my boyfriend. We told each other everything, but he didn't tell me the reason she was in jail. I never told anyone else. Well, not until now."

"Sue comes into the diner sometimes. I don't know her as well as my mother does, but I would hate to think she had anything to do with Silas's murder," I said. Sue didn't seem the murdering type, but sometimes people surprised you.

"I'm probably not thinking too straight right now, so maybe it's all my imagination. This whole thing has my mind in a mess. I just don't know what I'm going to do without him."

"You have every right to feel that way. Grief is something that's hard to deal with," I said sympathetically. "Karen, did Silas have any family in town?"

She shook her head. "No, his mother died several years ago, and he never knew his father. He has a sister, but she lives in Oregon. They didn't talk much. At Christmas time she would send him a card, and once every year or two he'd give her a call. He was really on his own in life, besides having me, that is. I mean, he had our co-workers and most of them had worked at the paper a long time, so there's that. Once in a while, someone would invite us over for a barbecue or dinner or something."

"No close friends? Someone he hung out with a lot?" I asked.

She shook her head again. "Not really. It was mostly just me. I've lost most of my close family too, so we spent most of our time together."

I felt sad when she said that. If she was virtually alone in this world, then she had just lost the only person that meant something to her. "I'm sorry. I wish there was something I could say to make things easier. If you need anything, I hope you'll let us know."

She smiled with tears in her eyes. "I appreciate that Rainey. You and your sister have always been so thoughtful."

Chapter Six

"WHAT WILL IT BE, COWBOY?" I asked as Cade took a seat at the front counter at Sam's Diner. His chocolate brown hair glimmered under the diner's fluorescent lighting.

"Cowboy?" he asked, tilting his head. "Do I look like I am, or have ever been, a cowboy?" The look of dismay on his face was priceless.

I looked him up and down in his bland gray suit. Nope. He could never be accused of looking like a cowboy. "I guess not. Do you know what you want?"

"I have really come to expect a higher level of service at this fine dining establishment. You're letting me down." He grinned.

"I don't know why you would expect that," I said, laying a menu on the counter in front of him. "We have a nice full pot of clam chowder, and with the weather cooling down like it has, it should be your first choice for lunch. Can I get you something to drink?"

"Iced tea would be great. Oh, and if you have those cute little oyster crackers, then I'd love some clam chowder."

I looked at him, one eyebrow lifted as a warning. "Cute little oyster crackers coming up."

I got him his iced tea and went to get the clam chowder. A big silver pot sat on the stove, simmering. "Man, that smells good, Sam," I said when I removed the lid. It was nowhere near my lunch break since I had the late shift, but my stomach growled. I was going to have to sneak a little something when there was a lull in customers or I'd faint from hunger. That's what you get when you rush out of the house without eating breakfast.

"It does smell good, doesn't it?" Sam said from his spot at the grill. Sam was my boss and the owner of the diner. He was a great guy to work for and he was currently flipping hamburger patties and hot dogs. "What did you make for us today?"

"Sorry, Sam, but I didn't bring anything in today," I said as I ladled out the chowder. "I made an apple crumb cake to take to Karen Forrest. Did you hear Silas Mills was killed?"

"I heard that. It's a shame. How's Karen taking it? I think they were together quite a while."

"They were, but I didn't know they'd been dating before Silas died. I guess they kept it quiet. She's having a tough time," I said and picked up the bowl of chowder and two packages of the oyster crackers. We normally served the clam chowder with saltines, but Sam had gotten some oyster crackers for his favorite customer several months earlier.

"Labor Day is going to be crazy around here, Rainey. I hope you don't have anything planned."

I sighed on my way out of the kitchen. "Not a thing, Sam."

I put the bowl of chowder down in front of Cade. "Nice and hot. Now, what have you figured out about Silas's murder?"

He looked at me, then picked up a package of crackers. "Depends. What do you know?"

I filled him in on what Karen had told me. It wasn't much, but it was all I had. As long as I stayed out of trouble, Cade didn't mind me asking around. It had taken him a while to see things my way and admit that I would be a help to him, but he had finally come to see things my way.

"And I think we should talk to Sue Hester, the owner of the boardinghouse," I finished.

He sat back in his chair, thinking about what I had told him. "Seems like a long shot. But you keep working on it," he said, giving me a wink.

I narrowed my eyes and put my hands on my hips, ready to give him my opinion on that when the diner door opened and Sue Hester stepped through it. I smiled at her when her eyes met mine, then I gave Cade a look.

"Good afternoon, Sue," I said, heading toward her. "Would you like a booth?"

She nodded, her brown eyes looking sad. "Yes, Rainey, thanks." I grabbed a menu when I passed the hostess station and led her to a booth in the corner, away from other diners, hoping I could get her to open up about Silas.

I took her drink order and brought back a glass of iced tea. "Do you need more time to decide?"

She looked up at me, laying the menu down. "I think I'd like a bowl of clam chowder. Sam makes the best around."

"You got it," I said, slowly writing up the ticket.

"I suppose you heard what happened to Silas Mills," she said in a lowered voice.

I looked up at her. She looked like she was about to cry. Sue had brown hair that had a few strands of gray in it and smooth skin that belied her true age. If I didn't know better, I might think she was in her late fifties or early sixties and not the seventy-plus years I knew her to be. "I did hear. It's such a shame. Didn't he live at your boardinghouse?"

She nodded. "For more than ten years. That place won't be the same without him. He was like a fixture of the place. I just don't understand it. I spoke to him the day he died and he seemed happy as could be. Not a care in the world."

"It's heartbreaking," I said and glanced over my shoulder. One of the other waitresses, Luanne, had the bulk of the tables so I turned back to Sue. "Did he seem different the last few days?"

She shook her head. "No, not really. The last day I saw him, we talked about the weather and his plans for the day. He said he was going to go see Karen Forrest. I don't know her well, but apparently, he might have had an interest in her. Other than that, I don't know what might have happened."

Might have had an interest in Karen?

"Oh, I thought they had been dating for a long time."

She stared at me blankly and then tears sprang to her eyes. "Oh, that's right. I forget sometimes," she said and smiled, blinking away the tears before they had a chance to fall. "I'm just so shaken by this. The poor thing. He was such a nice man. He'd help me out around the boardinghouse without me even asking him to."

"He sounds like a sweet person. I'm sure you knew him well after him spending ten years there." I wondered about what

Karen said about Sue spending some time in the penitentiary. I just couldn't imagine Sue being a hardened criminal.

She nodded. "I certainly did. I considered him a friend. A very good one. I just don't know what could have happened to him."

"Well, Cade is on the case. I'm sure he'll get things figured out," I said, hesitating before leaving her table. It seemed like she had more to say and I wanted to hear what it was.

"You know, Rainey, I do have my suspicions," she said after a moment and glanced to her left and then right. None of the closest tables had customers seated at them. "It's just that I have a boarder that had trouble with Silas. Or rather, Silas had trouble with him. Harry Adams. He's an older fellow, probably in his early eighties."

"What kind of trouble did Silas have with him?" I asked when she hesitated.

"They argued all the time. Harry is cranky and constantly complains about everything. Silas, he had a guitar and he would play softly at night. Oh, if you had heard him." Her eyes got a faraway look in them and she lit up at the memory. "The man had a real talent, I tell you. He could have been famous if he had wanted to be. But Harry, he complained bitterly about it. I had to tell Silas not to play late at night."

"I can see where playing guitar late at night might be a nuisance for some residents," I said, trying to sound neutral.

"Nonsense. Silas had such a gift. He played softly, and it made falling asleep easier. Really, Harry should have appreciated it. It can get hard to fall asleep when you're older. I mean, that's what I've heard. I guess we'll both know when we get there. But getting older is inevitable," she said knowingly. She sat up and straightened her blouse.

My eyes widened. "I guess some things get harder when you get older," I said. Did she think I thought she was somewhere near my age?

She nodded. "That's what I've heard. Anyway, that Harry is such a grumpy old thing. I guess that comes with age, too. Not that I'd know. But they had such terrible arguments. I told Silas I was going to give Harry an eviction notice so we would have some peace and quiet around there. But Silas was so sweet about it. He said he wouldn't hear of me kicking an old man out on the street and insisted I not do it."

"Really? That's nice of him since Harry seemed to have something against him. Did you ever speak to Harry about it?" I asked, sticking my order book into my pocket and glancing over my shoulder as more people came into the diner.

She nodded. "I did. He promised to behave himself, but of course, he didn't. They fought and fought. I told Silas that if he got tired of it, to let me know and I would evict him."

"What did they argue about, besides the guitar playing?" I asked. It sounded like living at the boardinghouse would have been a stressful situation.

"Anything and everything. Harry works at the newspaper as a janitor a few hours a week. It's not much, but I guess it keeps him active. Apparently, he didn't like some things Silas wrote in the paper. I don't know what. I think Harry was imagining things."

I nodded. The diner was filling up fast now, and I needed to get moving before my co-worker, Georgia Johnson, started hollering at me. She had issues with me. "Let me get you that clam chowder, Sue. I'll be right back."

Harry Adams had just moved to the top of my list of people I needed to talk to.

Chapter Seven

CADE WAS GONE BY THE time I finished with Sue and three other tables of customers. He never did tell me what he knew so far, but it was early in the investigation, so it wouldn't have surprised me if he said it wasn't much. What Sue said about Harry Adams was interesting. Was Harry just a grumpy old man that didn't like to fall asleep to the sound of a strumming guitar? Or did he have a beef with Silas that went deeper than that? I wouldn't exactly consider Harry and Silas coworkers when you took in the fact that Harry only worked a few hours a week as the janitor at the newspaper, so I couldn't imagine how there could have been a work squabble that had spilled over into their personal lives. But there might be something up with Harry and I needed to find out what.

When the diner finally closed, I brought a plastic tub full of dirty dishes into the kitchen to Ron White, our dishwasher. "I hate to do this to you Ron, but I gotta," I said as I set the tub on the counter near the sink.

"You're killin' me smalls," he said without turning around.

"So what are you making for us this week, Rainey?" Sam asked, turning to me from the grill. "I think I asked that earlier, and I didn't get an answer." He had rubber gloves on and was giving the grill the once over so it would be ready for tomorrow.

"I don't know. My mother suggested I make a birthday cake for mine and Stormy's birthday, so maybe I'll experiment with a recipe for cake," I said. My coworkers had gotten used to me bringing in food that I was creating for my new cookbook. It gave me lots of feedback and helped me develop my recipes. Sometimes Sam put the dishes on the menu for the customers to try out and give me their feedback.

"Remind me. When is your birthday?" he asked.

"September fifteenth."

"And I bet you'll want the day off?" he said with a grin.

I shrugged. "I don't know. It depends on if Cade can get the day off or not. With another murder, he may not be able to and I may as well work it."

"Seems like murders follow you around," Georgia grunted as she passed behind me and set her own tub of dirty dishes on the counter next to mine.

"I don't know what you mean by that," I said. Georgia and I had issues. I wasn't sure exactly what those issues were, but she enjoyed keeping them alive and well.

She smirked. "It just seems odd that since you moved back to Sparrow, people are dropping like flies."

I rolled my eyes. "Right. Like the people arrested for those murders are all innocent and I've been getting away with murder. I've got work to do."

I huffed away and went back to the dining room floor. Georgia wasn't worth the effort, and I wasn't going to waste my time fretting over what she said.

"Rainey, why is there another murder in town?" Luanne asked me, blinking her big brown eyes.

"How should I know?" I asked, wiping down a table.

"Georgia says you're suspicious."

I sighed. "Georgia's crazy. Listen, Luanne, did you happen to know Silas Mills?"

"Yeah, sure. He was my cousin's father-in-law. His daughter married my cousin John. I didn't know him well, but he showed up at family things once in a while. Mostly he kept to himself."

"Really? He had a daughter? Do you think your cousin would know anything about him or what might have happened?" I asked, turning to her. Sue had said Silas didn't have family, but Luanne was saying he had a daughter.

"I doubt it. He's dead. He had a terrible accident two years ago," she said and picked up a tub of dirty dishes and headed to the kitchen.

I bit my lower lip to keep from saying something unkind.

"SO, DON'T HOLD OUT on me," I said to Cade. "Tell me what you know about Silas." We were snuggled up on my loveseat, a pizza on a wooden crate in front of us, and the TV turned on to a romantic comedy.

"Not nearly enough. There was a raincoat in the dumpster out back and in the pocket was a cellphone that we're working on getting dried out and unlocked. I'm hoping it belongs to Silas, but I don't know for sure."

"A cell phone would be good. I bet it tells a lot. It would be even better if it belonged to the killer. Maybe they didn't realize their phone was in the pocket when they tossed it," I said and took a bite of the Hawaiian pizza on my plate.

"If it belonged to the killer, it would be fantastic, but it would be a miracle if it was. Although they may have tossed the raincoat if it had blood on it, and didn't realize the phone was in the pocket," he said and turned the channel to a football game.

"Hey," I said, giving him the eye.

"That movie was a rerun. You'll catch it the next time they run it," he said nonchalantly.

I sighed. "Maybe Silas got a text from the killer to meet him in my alley."

"I'm sure he did because alleys are where I always meet killers," he said with a smirk.

"You never know. What about those tire tracks? The big ones?" I asked him.

"I made a cast of them and picked up the silver pen and also picked up the trash from the dumpster."

"Trash from the dumpster? You're digging through it? Gross."

"I have a couple of officers looking through it right now, but yes, I'm taking a look at everything. Would you like to come down to the station and help sort it?"

"Nope. I think I'm going to pass on that one. Thanks for the offer though."

"Just thought I'd ask," he said. Maggie trotted in from the bedroom and stopped, staring at the two of us.

"Well, where have you been?" I asked her.

She yawned and her nose started twitching with the scent of the pizza.

"She missed the delivery guy. That dog can sleep," Cade said.

"Except when she's supposed to be sleeping. My neighbor isn't a fan. Maggie was out barking again early this morning," I said.

"Did you check and see what she was barking about?" he asked, tossing Maggie a piece of his pizza. Maggie caught it in mid-air, chewed twice and swallowed, wagging her tail. She sidled up to him, begging for more with those big brown eyes of hers and a soft whine.

"Sit, Maggie," I said. Maggie complied but kept her eye on Cade's pizza. "I didn't check to see what she was barking about, I just called her in. She came right away, so whatever it was, it must not have been that interesting. My neighbor caught me as I was getting into my car and complained about her again though."

"You make such an impression on people," he said.

"Smarty pants. I just can't imagine why Silas would be in my alley when he lived across town. Wouldn't he be closer to home if he was killed by someone local?"

He shrugged and tossed Maggie another piece of pizza. "Who knows? The killer may have brought him here and dumped him or he may have been killed out there. Maybe it's your cranky next-door neighbor? Did you ever think of that?"

I gasped. "I hadn't thought of that. He *is* cranky. Maybe Silas made him mad, and he killed him and dumped him behind my house."

"Maybe he's trying to get Maggie blamed so she'll get thrown into the slammer," he suggested.

"Maybe. I hate that we've got another murder on our hands," I said.

"Correction. I've got another murder on my hands. You're just digging around and not getting involved."

"Right," I said. But I needed an answer. Having a dead guy dumped behind my house made me feel like I needed to find the killer. Just in case someone seriously looked in my direction.

Chapter Eight

"WHAT KIND OF CAKE DO you want for our birthday, Stormy?" I asked as I measured flour into the bowl on the counter in front of me. I had been running through all kinds of options in my mind.

"I don't know. How about strawberry?" she said from the kitchen table. "And not fake strawberry. The real thing." She stirred more sugar into her tea.

"I can do strawberry. I think I'm going to make it a layer cake so we can each have our own flavor."

"I like key lime," Mom said, her feet up on a box that hadn't been unpacked yet.

"It's not your birthday. I'm thinking something like an orange chiffon for my layer," I said and poured vanilla extract into a measuring spoon. Vanilla was one of my favorite flavors, so I added double the amount the recipe called for.

"Or chocolate," Stormy said. "Natalie loves chocolate. But she said she can't come home for my birthday." With that, Stormy burst into tears.

I pulled a paper towel off the roll and handed it to her while Mom patted her shoulder.

"I know you're going to adjust to this," I promised her. "One day you'll be glad she's gone so you can turn her bedroom into your own private getaway."

She nodded, wiping her eyes. "I'm sorry. Bob says I need to stop this." The waterworks stopped as quickly as they started and she sniffed.

"It will get easier," Mom said. "When Rainey moved away to New York, I must have cried two whole days. Then I was over it. I just pretended you were her for a while and it worked. It helps to have identical twins."

"Thanks, Mom," I said and went back to my cake. "It's nice to know I can so easily be replaced."

"Aunt Rainey, I want cake," Lizzy announced, running into the kitchen. Lizzy was Stormy's youngest daughter. She and her sister Bonney were in the living room watching TV.

"It's not done yet, but I promise you will get some," I told her. She nodded, and ran back into the living room, her blond hair bouncing around her shoulders.

"Have you heard much about Silas Mill's murder?" Mom asked.

"Not a lot. Cade is still in the very beginning of the investigation," I said.

"I heard something," Stormy said.

We both turned to look at her. "And?" I asked.

"I heard he and Karen had a fight in the parking lot of the grocery store right before he died."

"How right before and who said it?" I asked.

"Susan Sardon said it," she said. "I used to work with her when I worked at the grocery store in high school. She still works there, and she was getting off work the night before Silas was killed. They were in the parking lot, arguing about him not making a commitment to her. She cried and said she was done with him and that she didn't ever want to see him again."

"Huh. That's odd since Karen said it was no big deal that he wouldn't marry her. She said she got used to them just being together," I said.

"Doesn't sound like she was used to it," Stormy said.

"I don't believe she would get used to it. I mean, it was twenty years. Come on. No woman wants to devote that kind of time to a guy that won't say yes," Mom said. "For goodness sakes, it's just marriage and if you've been with someone that long anyway, you may as well marry them."

"I thought the same thing when she told me," I said. "I didn't even know they were a couple. How do you keep that to yourself for so long?"

"You don't notice things, Rainey," Mom said.

"What do you mean I don't notice things? I'm practically a detective in my own right."

She laughed. "Sweet, innocent Rainey. Do you really think you're a detective? You didn't even notice when I threw all your holey socks out when you lived with me."

I rolled my eyes and ignored her. "Karen seems so quiet and keeps to herself. I can't imagine her killing someone. Especially someone she had such a long history with." I searched through my cabinet for a zester. I didn't have any oranges on hand, but I did have some lemons. They would do for now.

"Maybe Karen has a temper and she finally had enough of Silas not being able to commit?" Mom said. "Sometimes those quiet people aren't so quiet in their private lives."

"Could be," I said.

"What about Sue Hester? What did she say?" Stormy asked.

I wasn't sure how much I should tell them. My mother and sister were trustworthy, but I didn't want them to accidentally share something that might be sensitive in nature with someone that shouldn't hear it.

I shrugged. "Not a lot. She said Silas lived at the boardinghouse for more than ten years. Sometimes people there don't get along and I guess he may have had trouble from time to time. I think she's really going to miss him." I kept it light and free of pertinent details.

I washed two lemons and rolled them along the counter to loosen the juice inside of them.

"I can't imagine living in a boardinghouse. Do they have shared bathrooms?" Mom asked.

I glanced at her. "Ew. I didn't think to ask, but I couldn't live there if they do. I want my own bathroom."

"I want buttercream frosting," Stormy said. "With lots of vanilla."

"I was thinking of fondant. I want to experiment with marzipan decorations."

"I like buttercream," Stormy said.

I sighed. "I'll see what I can do."

"If I were looking for a killer, I'd check out that boardinghouse. Some of those people are suspicious looking. It's not like you get normal people in there," Mom said, and got up to make some tea.

"What do you mean normal? What's normal?" I asked her as I cut one of the lemons and squeezed it over a small bowl.

"You know what I mean. Drifters. People without roots to the community," she said, pouring water into a cup and putting it in the microwave.

"Silas lived there for ten years and worked at the newspaper. He had plenty of roots," I pointed out.

"I know, I know. But still," she insisted.

"You jump to conclusions," I said.

"Didn't Gary Haines live there years ago?" she said and shivered. "I always thought he was a murderer. I would have liked to know what he had in his basement back then."

I laughed. "You're terrible. Poor Gary was harmless. He was just odd." Gary Haines had a tendency to stare when he spoke to you, and then he'd continue staring for far too long after the conversation had ended.

"I think you should check out the boardinghouse," Stormy said. "I bet someone there has to know something. I mean, they lived together, ate together, and probably all talked to one another about personal stuff. Someone had to know something."

"You have a point there," I said. "I'm going to see if I can talk to people there."

"So, Cade doesn't mind you getting involved in his cases these days?" Mom asked, leaning against the kitchen counter.

"I don't know that he doesn't mind. I mean, he seems fine as long as I don't get into trouble."

The lemon smelled wonderful. I poured the juice into a small bowl that had melted butter in it and then began zesting the other lemon. I might change my mind about the orange and just go with lemon. It was a favorite of mine anyway.

"I like raspberry, too," Stormy said. "Raspberry cake would be good."

"What about Raspberry chocolate?" I asked, gently stirring in the lemon juice.

"Or raspberry white chocolate?" Mom suggested and removed a tea bag from the box on the counter.

"Now you're talking," I said. A raspberry white chocolate layer and a lemon layer would go together perfectly. "I can make it a triple layer cake and make the small layer on top vanilla in case anyone has allergies, or preferences."

"Like a wedding cake? How many people are coming to this party?" Mom asked.

I shrugged. "I don't know. Not many. There's Stormy's fi—four kids," I caught myself and glanced at Stormy. "And then a few friends. I want to invite Agatha, Cade, and maybe some people from work. It's a chance to show off my cake baking skills."

"Ulterior motives," Mom said.

"Maybe so," I said.

I needed to get over to the boarding house and see if anyone had any ideas on what had happened to Silas. Stormy was right. Someone there had to know something. I also hoped I could find Harry someplace I could speak to him alone. He and Silas had issues and I wanted to know what they were.

Chapter Nine

TWO DAYS LATER I STOPPED by the newspaper office. I had wanted to start up a subscription to the newspaper anyway, and I hoped to find Harry Adams there. With him only working a few hours a week, I thought it made sense that he might be there at the end of the day to clean up after everyone. If not, I would have to figure out some way of running into him. Meeting him at the boardinghouse would be my last resort. There would be too many people there that might overhear our conversation.

When I pulled up to the front curb, as luck would have it, there was an elderly gentleman cleaning the front windows of the newspaper office. The clock on my dashboard said two minutes to five. The newspaper closed at 5:30 so I had time to stop and talk to him before they closed.

"Oh my goodness, I'm not too late, am I?" I called out to the man as I headed to the door.

He turned and looked at me, questioning. "Eh?"

"Is the newspaper office closed?" I asked, giving him a big smile. "I just moved into my new house and I wanted to start up a subscription to the newspaper. Do you work here?"

"No. I just stop and clean any dirty windows that I find." He looked at me incredulously.

"Oh. Of course. Sorry." And then I stood and looked at him. I hadn't expected him to be so surly, but I should have if I'd paid attention to what Sue had told me. "I guess I should go inside, then."

He snorted and opened the glass door for me to enter. "Some people..." he muttered.

"Thank you," I said, feeling mildly stupid. I should have had a better plan of something to say if I wanted to get information out of him.

The desks inside the office were empty now, and I went to the front counter. The man came inside and began cleaning the inside of the plate-glass window. I wasn't sure what to do, so I walked up behind him and cleared my throat.

He looked over his shoulder at me. "What?"

"I was just waiting for someone to come to the front counter. It's a nice day, isn't it?"

He turned and looked at the clouds gathering in the sky outside and turned back. "I guess that depends on what your idea of nice is." He turned back to his work, leaving me standing there. I went to the window beside him.

"I guess we'll get some rain soon," I said.

He snorted again but didn't answer. I was sure he thought I was an idiot, but I didn't care.

"So, did you hear about the most recent murder? I don't know what's happening to Sparrow these days."

Now he turned toward me. "Doesn't surprise me a bit. That fool Silas Mills had it coming. The only surprise is, why didn't it happen sooner?"

"Oh? You knew Silas?" I asked.

He gave me another look that said he thought I was an idiot. "We both work for the newspaper."

I nodded. "Of course. I knew that. But, why doesn't it surprise you that he was killed?" Sue had one thing right. Harry was grumpy.

"Because he was always sticking his nose into other people's business. He was nothing but a troublemaker."

"What sort of trouble did he cause?" I asked, hoping he wouldn't get irritated with my questions. But he sounded like he wanted to complain about Silas, so I was going to be a listening ear.

"Told Sue Hester I was stealing from him. Is it my fault he misplaced his belongings? If he was responsible, he would have put them away to begin with," he said bitterly. "Like I would want his junk. I have no use for a journal or a cell phone. I lived all my years without them and I don't need them now."

"Silas's cell phone turned up missing?" I asked, thinking about the raincoat with the cell phone in its pocket.

He shrugged. "According to him and Sue Hester. I don't believe it though. He just wanted me kicked out of the boardinghouse. I never touched his junk."

"That sounds like an unpleasant place to live."

"Unpleasant isn't the half of it. He was always arguing with everyone. And then that idiot Charlie Rhoades moved in. After that, there was never any peace. Not to mention Silas was always playing that stupid guitar late into the night. With that racket going, no one got any sleep around there."

"Charlie Rhoades?" I asked. "Why did that cause problems?" I wanted to get his opinion on the trouble between Silas and Charlie.

"Because Silas wrote a nasty article about him a few years ago and he lost the election for city council." He gave me a sideways glance as he sprayed more window cleaner onto the glass. "Why do you care?"

I shrugged. "I guess I don't, but you know how it is in a small town. Everyone has a story about what happened. I bet it caused a lot of trouble if Silas wrote a negative article about Charlie and then Charlie lost the election."

He gave one curt nod of his head. "You better believe it. I told Sue not to let him move in. I also told her to get rid of Silas while she had the chance, but that woman had googly eyes for him so there was no convincing her."

"Googly eyes? What do you mean?"

He waved a hand. "Nothin'. That woman don't have good sense. Silas and Charlie Rhoades are cousins, you know."

"I had no idea," I lied. I knew Charlie from when he worked at the bookstore across the street from the diner. In a small town, we didn't have professional political candidates. They were usually regular citizens that wanted to hold office.

He nodded again and straightened up. "Yup. That woman don't have good sense." He walked away without another word and disappeared behind a closed door.

I wondered what he meant by Sue having googly eyes for Silas. Karen had said Sue was interested in Silas. Was there actually a relationship between them or was it all in her mind? I also wondered how bad things must have gotten with both Silas and his cousin Charlie, who had a grudge against him, living there. Add Harry and it sounded to me like that boardinghouse was probably a horrible place to live.

Another door opened and a young woman stepped out. When she saw me, she smiled. "I'm so sorry! I didn't hear anyone come in." She hurried to the front counter and picked up a pen. "What can I help you with?"

"It's okay, I know I'm coming in here at the last minute. I just wanted to get a subscription started for delivery of the newspaper," I said, walking up to the front counter. The woman looked familiar, but I wasn't sure where I knew her. Sometimes you saw the same people over and over in a small town and trying to place them took some thought.

"Well, let me have you fill out this short form and we'll get that started." She handed me a form and a pen and I began filling it in with my name and address.

"I think I'll sign up for six months," I said. "I guess you all must be going through a difficult time around here." I kept one eye on her as I wrote.

"What?" she asked.

"Silas?" I said.

"Oh, my gosh, yes. It's such a tragedy. I don't know who would have wanted to kill him." She shook her head sadly.

"I don't understand it, either," I said. "He seemed like such a nice guy. I work over at Sam's Diner and he would stop in sometimes."

"Oh, that's where I've seen you," she said, smiling again. "I knew you looked familiar. I stop in there when I can. Yes, Silas was a nice guy. Sometimes he could get crabby, but I guess we all have our days."

"We sure do," I agreed. "Did Silas only cover the local sports? Didn't he sometimes write other articles?"

"Sure, he filled in at other times, but mostly it was sports."

I nodded and signed the bottom of the form. "I guess you'll have to hire a new reporter?" It had suddenly occurred to me that I had writing experience and if there was an opening, it would help me pay for my house. Covering sports might be a challenge, but it would help me be less dependent on my mother. It might have been tacky so soon after Silas's death, but I was going to apply for a job.

"I think Bruce is going to fill his spot," she said.

"Oh, that's too bad. I was hoping you all were hiring. Not that that was the reason I was asking about Silas," I said, realizing that now I probably did sound tacky.

She smiled. "I think they're going to hire someone to write lifestyle articles, but just as a fill-in position, not a regular position. Did you want to submit an application?"

"That would be great!" I said too enthusiastically. "I've written several cookbooks and I'm in the middle of writing a new one now."

"That sounds great," she said reaching beneath the counter for a pad of applications. She pulled one off. "Sorry. We aren't fancy here. We still do it the old-fashioned, generic way." She laughed as she handed me the application.

"I don't mind at all," I said and paid for my subscription.

I left the newspaper office hoping for a new job and with just a little more information about Silas's life before he was murdered.

Chapter Ten

AFTER WORKING MY SHIFT at the diner and stopping by the newspaper office, I decided that a great big latte was in order. My friend Agatha Broome owned the British Tea and Coffee Company and sold the best coffee, tea, chocolate, and imported jams, jellies, and candies. She was a transplant from Britain and since it had been awhile since I had had the time to visit with her, I couldn't pass up the opportunity. The boardinghouse would have to wait for now.

"Hey Agatha," I said when I got to the front counter.

"Rainey! How are you today? Need a fill up with a latte and some chocolate?" she asked, her grin spreading across her face.

"You know I do. I think I want a pumpkin spice latte since we're almost into fall, and I'll skip the chocolate for now. I've been trying out cake recipes, and the testing has been showing up on my hips."

She laughed. "Nonsense! But I know how it is when you've got good food around. It's hard to stop," she said and began making my coffee. "I'll sit with you if you're going to stay awhile."

"That sounds great," I said. "How has business been?"

"It's been bustling, what with Labor Day weekend upon us."

The Snake River wound its way through our part of Idaho not far from Sparrow and we had a booming tourist business during the summer months. With Labor Day weekend beginning tomorrow, we would see a slowdown in tourists come Tuesday, but it wouldn't become dramatic until after it snowed. Even then, we would get people who rented the cabins on the far side of the river throughout the snowy months.

"I know, I have to work all weekend at the diner. I don't mind. It will be so busy I won't get a chance to wish I was off."

She finished making my latte and refused my payment. We went to a corner table to catch up. Agatha had short, curly white hair and wore gold-framed glasses. She looked like everyone's favorite grandma.

"Now then, tell me what you're up to? How's the cookbook coming?" She stirred the cup of tea she had made for herself and looked at me expectantly.

"The cookbook is going great. I've been working on cake recipes this week."

"And don't you and Stormy have a birthday coming up soon?" she asked.

"We certainly do. We'll be having a small get together on the fifteenth and we would love for you to attend," I said and took a sip of my latte. "Mmm. Perfect, as always."

"Thank you, love. I would love to come to your party. I suppose our handsome and fearless Detective Cade Starkey will be attending?" she asked with a grin. "That lad's a keeper, I tell you."

I felt my cheeks go pink. I couldn't help it. She just might be right about Cade. "I'm sure he will be, but he might be late. He's working on another case. Did you hear about Silas Mills?"

She nodded. "I did. It's not that big of a surprise if you want to know the truth."

"Seriously? Why do you say that?" I asked.

She shrugged. "There was just something about him. He looked like a rough character and if I hadn't known he worked for the paper, I would have kept an eye on him when he came in here to get a coffee."

She had a point. Silas did look like he had lived a rough life, but I couldn't say that I had heard much about him. Like Karen, he seemed to keep to himself. "Do you know anything specific?"

"I don't know anything specific, exactly. He just had a way about him. I wouldn't be surprised if Cade discovers he was up to no good and someone got tired of it and took care of him. But I do know he was two-timing Karen Forrest." We looked toward the door when it opened. A young couple walked in and went to the front counter. "Susie will take care of them."

"Who was he two-timing with?" I whispered.

"Sue Hester."

"Seriously? Sue Hester?" That explained why she had practically swooned when I spoke to her about Silas the other day. But she had failed to mention the fact that she had been dating Silas. "Do you know that for a fact?"

She nodded. "I saw them out together myself. Over in Boise. It's been about six months ago, so who knows if they were still seeing one another more recently."

"It's funny she forgot to mention that when I talked to her the other day. She said they were friends. He had lived at her boardinghouse for more than ten years."

"Doesn't surprise me. I don't mean to say anything unkind about Karen, but she was a fool for staying with him so long. I think he wouldn't marry her because of Sue. Although, I do wonder if he knew how much older Sue is. She likes to pretend she isn't as old as she is."

I nodded. "She does look much younger than she is. I guess if you can make people think you're younger, then go for it."

She giggled. "You've got a point there. I wish I could do it myself, but these wrinkles are getting deeper by the day."

"Oh, stop it. Those are laugh lines and they make you beautiful," I said. I meant it. Agatha had the prettiest skin of anyone I knew.

She laughed harder. "I need you to stick around. You're good for my ego."

We both laughed.

"Rainey?"

I looked up to see my ex-husband, Craig Strong, standing at our table. How had he come in without us noticing him? He looked at me, and then at Agatha. Agatha's eyes went to mine, expectantly.

"Craig," I said and looked at Agatha. "Agatha, this is my ex-husband, Craig Strong." I didn't really want to introduce them, but it was rude not to.

"Oh, so this is the infamous Craig Strong," Agatha said, sitting back in her chair and looking him up and down.

Craig's eyes went wide. He glanced at me, then turned to her. "Yeah, it's me," he said weakly. "Nice to meet you."

She laughed. "Don't mind me. I'm giving you a hard time. I better get behind the counter. Susie's getting a bit of a line." She got up and glanced over her shoulder at Craig before going to help her assistant.

Craig sat down without asking. "How are you doing, Rainey?"

I sighed. "I'm doing great, Craig. What do you want?" I wasn't trying to be rude to Craig. I was just done with him hanging out in Sparrow. It had been a nasty divorce, and I had hoped to leave him and all my troubles behind in New York City, but he had followed me here with the news that he had an inoperable brain tumor. As much as I hated to hear he was dying, I hoped he would find some place else to go soon.

He forced a smile. "I'm doing well. I just thought I'd stop in and get some coffee and I happened to see you here at the table." He shrugged as if that was explanation enough.

"Okay. Well, I need to be getting home. I'm bushed. My feet ache and I'm ready to take my shoes off." I made a move to stand up, but he stopped me.

"Rainey, I really was hoping we could get along better," he said, sounding hopeful.

Craig had nearly destroyed me in the divorce and he *had* destroyed my career. Forgiving him was going to take some time, but one good thing came out of his appearing in Sparrow. I had been able to leave the past behind and move forward with a relationship with Cade.

"I don't want to be cruel, Craig. But I don't want to be friends. I meant it when I said I was sorry you're dying. I really did. But, I think that has to be the end of it."

He was quiet, taking this in. "I guess I don't blame you. Will you forgive me? I mean, really forgive me?"

"With time, I will. When are you going back to New York?" I asked.

"I have a doctor's appointment next week, so I guess I'll be leaving then."

I nodded. I wanted to say more, and I hated myself for feeling like I owed it to him just because he was dying. I didn't owe him anything. I sighed.

"I do hope for the best for you." And when I said it, I realized that I meant it.

Chapter Eleven

I FILLED CADE IN ON what I had found out regarding Silas's murder the previous evening and he did what he usually did. He told me almost nothing that he knew. To be sure, he appreciated what I found out, but when I asked for details, all I got was a grin. He did say he had interviewed Karen Forrest and Sue Hester, but he didn't elaborate. That's what I got for dating a detective. He kept things to himself.

I was undaunted though. I would find out who killed and dumped Silas Mills behind my house on my own. My alley was not going to be a dumping ground for dead bodies. Or at least, I didn't want it to become one.

I had spent a sleepless night going over everything I had heard about the murder and one of the things that stood out was the fact that Silas had written that article about his cousin Charlie Rhoades, and it cost him a seat on the city council. After working the morning shift at Sam's, I stopped in at Charlie's Hobby Shop. Charlie Rhoades had opened the shop up about six months earlier and I was hoping to get some information out of him about his relationship with Silas.

"Good morning, Rainey," Charlie said when I walked in the door.

I hesitated for a moment, not recognizing Charlie. He had put on weight since I last saw him and the long, full beard he was sporting surprised me. He didn't seem the type to grow one. "Hi Charlie, how are you?"

"Can't complain," he said with a grin and came out from behind the counter. "What brings you to my little shop?"

"I've been intending to stop in and see what all you carried," I said. The shop walls were lined with shelves that looked homemade and they were sparsely filled with an assortment of merchandise.

"I've got all kinds of things. Games, puzzles, models, collectibles and accessories, and radio controlled cars and trains. I try to stay away from the video games since I was going for more of a retro-type hobby shop. But I do carry all sorts of collectible characters from video games."

There were swords and daggers on one wall and a shelf full of comic books on another. "You sure do have a variety of merchandise in here," I said, looking around. Although there was a variety of merchandise, there wasn't a lot of it and I wondered if he would be able to compete with larger stores.

"I do try to keep a lot of items in stock," he said proudly. Charlie wore a blue plaid shirt that opened further down in front than was necessary and wiry gray chest hair poked out of the front of the shirt.

"It's good to see new businesses open up in Sparrow. How has it been going?" I asked, walking over to a shelf that held small figurines and action figures. My nephews played video games all the time, but now that I was standing in front of the action figures, I couldn't remember exactly which games they were into.

"I guess you could say things are going okay," he said hesitantly. "Are you interested in any of these?" He picked up a *Harry Potter* figurine. "I just got these in. People are still really into *Harry Potter*."

"I'm sure Harry is destined to become a classic," I said. "I know my nephews like playing video games, but I forget which ones."

He nodded. "There's a lot out there. Maybe it's *Halo* or *Tour of Duty*?" He held up some action figures but they didn't look familiar.

"I'll probably get into trouble if I pick something up without them being here to tell me exactly which they want. They are very particular about their collectibles."

"Most people are. Let me tell you, trying to sell someone something that isn't what they are into is almost impossible."

"I bet it is," I said and walked over to the wall that held swords and daggers. "Do these sell?"

"Oh, sure. Those do very well. If you'd like to look at anything, I'll get it down for you."

I nodded. I wouldn't want my nephews to have one, but I was sure they would like them. "It sure is a shame that Silas Mills was murdered, isn't it?" I said casually. "Sparrow seems to have a lot of trouble with that kind of thing lately."

His mouth formed a hard line, and he wiped his hands on his shirt without looking at me. "I don't know if I'd call it a shame exactly. People like Silas Mills are nothing but trouble and it's just as well that we're free of him."

I turned to him, putting a surprised look on my face. "Oh? Why do you say that?"

"He was my cousin and I guess I know a thing or two about him," he said, taking a step back.

"I guess I had forgotten that. I'm still sorry he died. Someone somewhere cared about him."

He snorted. "That guy," he said shaking his head and pausing before continuing. "He was always trying to cause trouble, and not just in the family. Anywhere he could cause trouble, he did."

I considered this a moment. "Charlie, don't you live down at Sue's boardinghouse? And didn't Silas live there, too?"

He nodded. "I still do and he did. He caused trouble for people there, too. Always arguing with them and then telling one person one thing and another something else. People were at each other's throats all the time because of him."

"That sounds like a big mess. How long have you lived there?" I asked and picked up a dagger with a jeweled handle for something to do. The jewels were cheap colored plastic and had been glued onto the handle.

"I've been there a little over a year. I was looking for someplace else to live because of Silas, but I guess I don't have to bother now that he's gone." He smiled.

"It was that bad down there?"

He nodded. "Oh, yeah. For example, he went to Sue and told her that old Harry was stealing food from the kitchen at night and that made Sue mad at Harry. I doubt very seriously that Harry did anything of the sort. He's a grumpy old guy, but he isn't a thief. Silas told Sue that just because he could. Shoot, a few years ago when I was running for city council, he wrote an article saying I had ties to organized crime." He snorted and shook his head. "Ridiculous!"

"Wow. I can't imagine why someone would say something like that," I said, hanging the dagger back up on the wall.

"Silas was twisted. That was the real issue."

"Why did you move into the boardinghouse then? Silas had lived there a long time before you moved in, didn't he? I mean, you knew that, right?"

"Oh, yeah. He'd been there for years. I didn't want to move in there, but it was the cheapest place in town. I lost my job from the bookstore and I needed something I could afford. They had a lot of layoffs down there, you know? It's not like I was fired." He glanced away.

I nodded. "That happens sometimes. I guess it makes things hard when you have a major life change like that."

He cleared his throat before answering. "I told Sue she needed to kick Silas out. He caused trouble with everyone down there at some point or other, but she wouldn't do it. They had a thing going on, you know?"

I turned to him. "Silas and Sue? I thought Silas and Karen Forrest had been seeing each other for years?"

He grinned. "Oh, yeah. But Sue and him were sneaking around for years, too. I heard Karen wanted him to marry her but he wouldn't because he was seeing Sue on the side. I can't imagine why he was since she was so much older than him and she was just very different from him, but I saw her sneaking out of his room late at night a couple of times."

Harry had said Sue had googly eyes for Silas. Maybe she had more than that. "Poor Karen. I hope she doesn't know about that. It would break her heart after being with him for so long."

He chuckled. "Oh, Karen knew all right. They had terrible fights over it. One time, right after I moved in, the three of them stood out on the front porch, all of them screaming at each other. It was awful, and I thought I was going to have to call the cops to break it up."

"Oh, wow," I said. "That's not what you want to have happen right after you just moved into a new place. I bet it made you rethink the move."

"You better believe it. But, Karen isn't a girl scout herself, you know. She had someone on the side, too. That boardinghouse is a regular *Peyton Place*."

I stared at him. "I never would have guessed that. I never hear of any trouble there."

"I guess you just got to ask the right people. Trust me. Silas Mills got what he had coming to him."

"Who was Karen seeing?"

He shrugged. "I don't know. I just heard it from enough people to know it's true."

I was surprised about the things Charlie was saying. All three of them out on the front porch fighting must have been quite a scene. Either Karen or Sue would have had good reason to kill Silas.

Chapter Twelve

"EXCUSE ME, DEAR," I heard a voice behind me say.

I straightened up from the planter I was weeding and looked over my shoulder to see who it was. "Oh, hello," I said to the elderly woman standing in front of me. Or rather, behind me. I turned to face her.

She smiled, her white hair was pulled back into a bun and her orange sweatshirt declared fall had arrived in patchwork letters amidst appliqued brown and gold leaves. "My name is Ida Snow, I live next door. I noticed you moved in last week. I hope you'll forgive me for not coming over sooner, but I was feeling under the weather."

"Oh, I'm sorry to hear that, I hope you're feeling better now," I said removing my gardening glove and sticking my hand out to shake hers. "I'm Rainey Daye. Excuse my mess, I've been pulling weeds and cleaning up the yard today." A pile of dead and mangled weeds lay at my feet as we spoke, and I brushed the dirt from the front of my shirt.

"This house was empty for nearly a year. I bet you have all kinds of work to do, don't you?" she asked pleasantly.

"You can say that again," I agreed. "I know the leaves are going to be falling soon and I'll have to rake again, but I couldn't wait another minute to get these weeds out."

I had survived the three day Labor Day weekend and as a result, I had a day off of work at the diner to work on my yard. My back already ached, and I wished I had stayed on the couch and watched TV instead, but I knew the results on my yard would be worth it.

"I think you've already met my husband?" she asked with a twinkle in her eye.

I forced myself to smile. "I sure did. I apologize for my dog being a nuisance. I think she just needs to settle into her new home, and then she'll be less noisy."

"Nonsense, I hardly noticed. Don't pay attention to Burt. He gets a bit grumpy from time to time, but if you do what I do, you'll get along fine with him."

"What do you do?"

"Ignore him." She tilted her head back and laughed.

I chuckled. "I'll keep that in mind." I had the feeling that if I tried to ignore Burt, he wouldn't let me get away with it like Ida could.

"Have you lived here in Sparrow long?" she asked.

"All my life, except for the ten years I was married. I lived in New York then, but I moved back earlier this year after I got divorced."

"Burt and I have been married sixty years. It's not always easy, but you get along somehow."

I wasn't going to explain to her where my marriage went wrong. She was from another generation and as much as I admired a couple's ability to stick things out, there were some marriages that were not worth being saved.

"It's such a lovely neighborhood," I said. "I feel like I won the lottery when I bought this house."

She nodded. "I've lived in Sparrow all my life. I still love this town, although things haven't been quite the same in recent years. I don't know what's going on around here. Did you hear Silas Mills was murdered, and they found his body right out in our alley? I never would have dreamed something like that could happen around here."

"I did," I said. "It's a terrible shame."

She shook her head and made a clucking sound. "I feel sorry for Harry Adams. It's a shame indeed."

"Why do you say that?" I asked, leaning against my porch railing. I was pretty sure Harry Adams was relieved that Silas was gone.

"He was Silas's father. Not that anyone much knows that. Harry never wanted anything to do with him when he was younger, but when Harry tried to start up a relationship with him in his later years, Silas didn't want anything to do with him. It's a sad case."

I was stunned. "Harry is Silas's father? How do you know that?"

"I went to school with Harry and Silas's mother was my best friend. Back then it was a terrible scandal when a girl was with child and unmarried. Susan went away to an unwed mother's home and had the baby. The nuns tried to get her to give the baby up for adoption, but she refused and brought him home here to Sparrow."

"How did she support him when she moved back? I would imagine it would be hard for an unmarried woman to support a child on her own back then."

"That's the truth. Things were hard. People weren't accepting of what she had done. Back then we had a clothing factory here in Sparrow where shirts and dresses were made and Susan got a job there. Her mother took care of Silas while she worked. That clothing factory was hard work and little pay, but the people were nice to work for. I worked there for a while when Burt was in the army. It helped to make ends meet. But Harry went off to the navy and didn't move back to Sparrow until a few years ago."

"So did Harry have any contact with Susan while he was in the navy?" I asked.

"Oh no. Susan wrote letter after letter to him. Harry's cousin finally told her he had married another woman when he got out of the navy. Susan gave up trying to contact him after that," she said. A dark cloud crossed over the sun threatening rain, and we both looked up.

"That's a shame. I'm sure it was hard for Susan. Does she still live around here?"

"No, she passed away a few years ago. Cancer. But when Harry came back to town, he looked Silas up. When he found out Silas lived at the boardinghouse, he rented a room there, too," she said pleasantly.

It seemed odd that Harry would move into the boardinghouse when from what everyone else said, the two didn't get along.

"Did Silas know Harry was his father when he moved in?" I asked.

"Oh, sure. Harry told me that he told Silas, but Silas wanted nothing to do with him. It broke Harry's heart, but it's not like you can blame Silas. His mother worked hard and made a lot of sacrifices to support him when he was young. When Silas was six, she married Joseph Mills, and he took on his last name. But, they were poor and Susan always had to work. She never got to be a stay at home mother like most women were back then."

"I wonder why Harry stayed at the boardinghouse if Silas didn't want him there? I would think when Silas rejected him, he wouldn't have moved in there."

She shrugged. "I guess Harry thought he could change Silas's mind. The last time I spoke to Harry, which was about two weeks ago, he had been angry. He said he never should have tried to contact Silas, and he wished he hadn't moved into the boardinghouse. But, money is tight when you live on a fixed income and he didn't have the money to move out."

That must be why he took the job as the janitor at the newspaper, I thought. "I wonder how Harry's doing now that Silas has been murdered? It might make him bitter for what he lost," I said.

"It wouldn't surprise me. Harry cussed Silas when I spoke to him last. Said he hated him. But I happen to know that hurt can hide behind anger. I've experienced it a few times. I don't believe for one minute that he hates Silas, but I bet now he regrets not being a father to Silas when he was younger."

"I bet he does," I agreed.

Cade had said he thought Silas's murder was a crime of passion. Perhaps it was a crime committed by a father rejected and frustrated by a son that he never got a chance to really get to know.

"Well, I hate to keep you. I know you have a lot of work to get done. I need to get Burt to working on our yard. He hates yard work," she said and laughed. "Now, don't you be a stranger. You come on over anytime you want and don't let Burt scare you off. He's grumpy, but he means well. And when he gets to know you better, he'll soften right up."

"I'll do that. It's nice meeting you, Ida. You stop by anytime you'd like," I said. I thought I was going to like living next door to Ida. The jury was still out on whether I would enjoy living next door to Burt.

I watched her go and wondered about Harry. It would have been a deep blow to have Silas reject him after he moved into the boardinghouse. All the bickering may have been from anger and bitterness coming from both sides.

Chapter Thirteen

"HELLO, RAINEY, HOW are you?" Karen asked me. Her hands were folded together on top of a big oak desk in her office at the newspaper.

"I'm great, Karen. Are you doing my interview?" I asked and took a seat at one of the visitors' chairs in front of the desk. I had gotten a call to come in and interview for the position at the newspaper and I was surprised to see Karen at the desk.

She nodded, barely able to suppress a grin. "Yes. I just got a promotion to personnel. I'll still be writing a few articles and handling some of the advertising like I always have, but since Silas is gone, there has been some shifting of positions."

"That's wonderful, congratulations!" I said. I was surprised to see Karen so happy even if she did just get a promotion. Her longtime boyfriend had just been murdered, after all.

"Thanks! I saw your application on top of the application pile and I just had to talk to you. I already know you're qualified with all the writing you've done in the past. I think your mom mentioned you were writing a new cookbook?"

"Yes, I'm working on an Americana themed cookbook. I'm hoping to have it ready by early next year," I said. "I was told the position was for a lifestyle article writer?"

She nodded. "Yes, among other things. We may need the person we hire to fill in with other departments and maybe go out to locations and do interviews. It all depends on what's going on around town. Does that sound like something you'd be interested in?"

"It does. I just bought a house and I can use the work. Mom helped me get into the house but I don't want to be dependent on her if I can help it," I said.

"Well, I have to interview more people, but between you and me, if I can get approval from our publisher, Walt Jones, I'd like to hire you."

I smiled, relieved. She filled me in on the details including the pay, which wasn't much, but would still help. I looked around the room. There were old bookcases along the wall that looked like they had been there since the newspaper started up. On the shelves were old, tattered books, crowded together.

"So do you like working here?" I asked. "Haven't you been here a long time?"

"Since right after graduating from the junior college. It's a nice place to work. Sometimes Walt can be cantankerous, but don't let him scare you. He's a nice guy with a big heart."

"I'll keep an eye out for him, then."

"Oh, and keep an eye out for our janitor, Harry Adams," she said and chuckled. "He's a grumpy one, but he doesn't bite. Or at least, not often."

"Will do," I said, leaning back in my chair. "I'm getting excited just thinking about the possibility of working at the newspaper."

She nodded. "I think you'll like it," she said, then became thoughtful a moment. "Say, Rainey, I know you're dating Cade Starkey. Has he mentioned anything about Silas's murder? It's been almost two weeks, and I was hoping to at least hear something by now."

"He's kind of tightlipped about that, if you want to know the truth. But I know he'll get to the bottom of it soon," I said. "You know, Karen, someone mentioned that Silas had a daughter, but I thought you said he really didn't have much family?"

She sighed. "That would be Annie. Yes, he has a daughter all right, but in name only, really. They never got along and she moved to Wyoming or Nevada, I can't remember which, and she hadn't spoken to him in years."

"That's really sad. What about her mother? Was Silas married to her?"

"No, he never married. Annie's mother has been out of the picture for so long, I can't even remember her name. She raised Annie to hate Silas, so that's why she didn't have much to do with her father," she said, fiddling with the pen on her desk.

"That really is sad," I repeated. It was odd that Karen had forgotten about Silas's daughter, even if she was out of the picture for the most part. "Have you heard anything going around town about his murder?"

"No, not a thing. It's kept me up late at night," she said. "The more I think about things, the more I think Silas's cousin, Charlie Rhoades, may have had something to do with his death."

My antenna went up. "Why do you say that?"

She leaned in closer. "When Silas wrote that article on him a few years ago, Charlie went nuts. He came down here, shouting at Silas, threatening him. He told him he would pay him back when he least expected it. Walt had to call the police to get him out of the office. He just wouldn't leave on his own."

"He was going to pay him back?" I asked. "How long has it been since this happened?"

"I think it's been around three years. I'd have to look up that article Silas wrote to be sure."

"That's a long time for him to wait to pay him back," I said.

She shrugged. "I guess it is. But I distinctly remember him saying it would be when he least expected it. Personally, I think he waited until he thought people had forgotten his threat. But Silas never forgot. We just talked about it a month ago."

"Why did it come up a month ago?" I asked her.

"Silas was having a hard time with Charlie living at the boardinghouse. Someone broke into his room and rifled through his belongings and then squirted ketchup on his clothes."

"Seriously? Ketchup? Sounds kind of childish."

"I think it was a threat. He wanted to scare Silas. Silas thought it had to be Charlie. No one else would be able to do it, nor would they care to," she said, sitting back in her chair.

I thought this over. I supposed the ketchup could have been symbolic of blood, but it seemed juvenile to me. "Did he report it to the police? Or to Sue Hester?"

She shook her head. "He didn't want to tell the police, but he did tell Sue. He said he confronted Charlie, too, but he denied it. Sue said she didn't know who would do such a thing, and she had the door replaced."

"The door was damaged in the break-in? Who was in the boarding house when it happened?"

"It happened during the day when Silas was at work. Sue had left to do the shopping for meals at the boarding house and those that worked were gone. There were only a couple of older folks there. Neither of them heard a thing, but they never do. They're hard of hearing. Whoever did it forced the door open with something. Silas didn't want to report it to the police because he had been having trouble with the lock and had forgotten to mention it to Sue. He said it wouldn't have taken a lot to get it open if he hadn't made sure he pulled it closed tight enough, and he thought he may not have been careful that morning."

"That's interesting. Did they take anything from his room?"

"Just a couple of journals. Being a writer, Silas always kept one. They took the one from last year and the current one. He had a hundred dollars in one of the drawers of his dresser, but they didn't take that."

Harry had said Silas told Sue that he had stolen the journals and a cell phone. I suddenly had a picture of everyone at the boardinghouse accusing one another of stealing.

"So, nothing else in the boardinghouse was damaged or broken into?" I asked.

She shook her head. "Nothing. Whoever it was, they came looking for him."

"Did you mention it to Cade? It's something he really needs to know."

"I completely forgot. I don't know how I did that," she laughed nervously when she said it and it made me wonder about her. I would have expected more grief, but she had conducted the interview in a lighthearted manner.

"If you don't mind, I'll mention this to Cade. I'm sure he'll be interested. Can anyone off the street walk into the boardinghouse? Is there some kind of security there?" I asked.

"It's pretty open. I doubt Sue would have security there. She's not someone that is very up on things like that and I don't remember Silas ever mentioning it. I didn't even think to ask him when he told me about someone breaking into his room. I guess I don't think sometimes, but he was sure it was Charlie, and it didn't amount to anything."

"It must have been hard for the two of them to get along together at the boardinghouse." It still didn't make sense to me that Charlie would move in when he knew Silas lived there, even if it was the cheapest rent in town. If it were me, I would have gotten another job to keep from having to live so near someone I couldn't stand.

"They argued all the time. Sometimes Charlie would block the path in the hallway and refuse to let Silas pass," she said and pushed her glasses further up on her nose.

"Why did Silas stay there? I don't want to pry, but why didn't he move in with you?"

Her cheeks went pink, and she laughed nervously again. "I told him he could. But, he said no one was going to bully him and force him out of his home. It didn't make sense to me, either. I tried to get him to move in." She gave the same nervous laugh again, and it made me wonder about their relationship.

"Well, thanks for the information. I'll let Cade know and I'm sure he'll have some more questions for you."

She nodded. "I'll be back in touch with you about the job as soon as I get the okay from Walt. Oh, but don't mention it to anyone yet. There are other people I need to interview."

"No problem, Karen. I'll keep it to myself. I do appreciate this!"

I left the newspaper office feeling like there were still a lot of unexplained things about Silas's and Karen's relationship. And who would break in and squirt ketchup on his clothes? It did sound childish, but Karen might be right about Charlie, especially since the money hadn't been stolen.

Chapter Fourteen

THE DOOR SWUNG OPEN and Cade walked through it looking like a breath of fresh air. He smiled when he saw me. "Good morning, Rainey."

"Good morning, Cade." I couldn't help but smile back. Then I giggled. "What can I get you, Cade? Scrambled eggs and toast?" Cade was a bit predictable with his food choices. I didn't mind. It made things easier.

"It's like you read my mind," he said with a grin and took a seat at the diner counter.

I got him a cup of coffee and then turned in his order.

"What do you know?" I asked when I got back to him. He had remained tight-lipped about the investigation long enough and I wanted to know what was going on.

"Are things a little slow in here?" he asked, looking around the diner. "There's usually a lot more people in here this time of day." Sam's was only open for breakfast and lunch and he was right. It was breakfast time, and we didn't have many customers.

"Things slow down a bit when summer ends, but it'll pick up again. Don't ignore my question."

"You tell me what you know, first," he said.

I filled him in on the details that I had collected, including the break-in of Silas's room at the boardinghouse.

"Why didn't someone tell me that earlier?" he asked, sounding exasperated.

I shrugged. "Silas thought it was nothing and told Karen and Sue that. But now Karen thinks it was Charlie that did it to scare him, and that he killed Silas."

"I guess it could have been. It would have been nice to know this earlier. We went through Silas's room, but there wasn't a lot there. He didn't have many possessions. We didn't look at fingerprints because we didn't know there had been a break in. Of course, there have been people in there before his death and I'm sure afterward as well. Sue and Karen for sure."

"What else do you have?" I asked him. "I know you have to know something by now."

He shrugged. "We're waiting for the fingerprints to come back on the knife and our IT guy hasn't unlocked the phone yet. So, not a lot."

I studied him. Was he holding out on me? I thought he was, but pushing Cade never worked. I had to be subtle if I wanted to get something out of him.

The front door opened and Mom stood there. When she saw Cade sitting at the front counter, she grinned.

"Well, good morning Detective Starkey!" she nearly shouted.

He turned and smiled. "Good morning, Mrs. Daye. How are you on this lovely morning?"

"Fantastic now that I've gotten a chance to see you, along with my unwed daughter."

"Mom!" I hissed.

Cade's shoulders shook from the laughter he was holding back. "Mrs. Daye, you have a lovely daughter," he said with a bad cockney accent.

"I have two lovely daughters, but one is married. You can have this one."

I sighed. "Stop it." I handed her a menu.

"Rainey, I need you to cater a party I'm having," Mom said as she opened the menu and laid it flat on the front counter.

I cocked an eyebrow. "What kind of party?"

"A birthday party," she said, not looking up from the menu. She slipped her reading glasses on, but still didn't look up.

I sighed. "And whose birthday party might this be?"

"Yours and Stormy's," she said. "How are the pancakes here?"

"You know how the pancakes are. You've eaten them hundreds of times," I said pulling my order book from my apron pocket.

She looked up at me and narrowed her eyes. "Are you trying to say something about my weight?"

"What? No. I just meant that you've eaten here a lot."

This didn't appease her. "Define 'a lot'."

"No, I will not define 'a lot'. Do you want the pancakes?" I asked.

"I'm going to have a talk with Sam about you. And yes, I'd like an order of pancakes," she said and brushed at imaginary lint on her blouse.

"One tall stack coming up," I said, jotting the order onto my pad and heading to the kitchen. I left mom at the counter, mumbling something about smart-alecky daughters. "One more for you, Sam."

He turned from the grill and glanced at the order I clipped to the order holder.

"Pancakes. My favorite," he said. "Hey Rainey, where's that birthday cake you promised? You know we've all got to give it a try and weigh in with our opinion on it."

"You and my mom, both," I said. "I'll bring some soon." I turned and headed back to the diner counter.

Mom was regaling Cade with a story from my childhood when I got back to them.

"So, when am I going to be asked out on another date?" I asked him.

He smiled. "I thought you were a modern woman? Why don't you ask me?"

"Would you like to have dinner at my house tomorrow night?" I asked him.

"I would love it," he said. "I'm tired of frozen dinners."

"I hear Sue Hester serves meals when you rent a room from her, and there's an opening," Mom said.

His eyes went wide. "Why, Mary Ann, I didn't know you had a mean streak in you."

"You'll learn," I said.

"Rainey's a mean girl, too," Mom advised him.

"I think I can see where she might have gotten it from," he said.

"Don't pay attention to her," I advised him. "She's the original Mommy Dearest."

"I hate to break up the family reunion," Georgia said, walking behind me and heading toward the kitchen. "But there are other customers in here."

Cade lifted an eyebrow. "You better get to work."

I rolled my eyes. "She thinks she's the boss."

I STOPPED OFF AT THE grocery store after work. I wanted to pick up some more lemons, raspberries, and cake flour among other things. I was reasonably sure I had the cake recipe down pat, but I wanted another go at it before the big day. I didn't mind doing my own cooking for my birthday. It was something I truly enjoyed.

There was a tall, thin woman placing apples into a bag when I got to the produce section. When she turned around, I realized it was Sue Hester.

"Hi, Sue," I said as I sidled up to her. I could always use apples.

"Well, hello, Rainey. It is Rainey, isn't it?" she asked, squinting at me. "I left my glasses at home and it's hard enough telling you from your sister when I have them with me."

"You got it right," I said, chuckling. "It's Rainey. How are you?"

She frowned. "Oh. You know how it is. The boardinghouse isn't the same without Silas around. You never know how much you depend on a person until they aren't around anymore."

"You relied on him to help you a lot?" I asked sympathetically.

She nodded. "Not just to help with things around the boardinghouse, like changing light bulbs or fixing minor things that had broken, but just his company."

That made me wonder about her. Was Charlie right when he said she and Silas were having an affair? "It's nice that you were so close, though I know it's terrible to lose someone. I try to tell myself the pain I feel when someone dies is a reflection of how much I cared for them while they were still alive."

She looked at me, her eyes wet with unshed tears. "That is exactly how it is. You got it exactly right."

"So, has Silas's next of kin come to collect his things from his room?"

She looked at me and blinked. "No. I don't think Silas had any next of kin, his things are still in his room. He's paid up until the beginning of next month. If someone doesn't contact me about it, I guess I'll have to figure out something to do with all his things. I can hardly stand to go through it, and I don't know what I'd do with it anyway. It's not like I can just throw it out."

"Karen didn't come and get it?" I asked. I would have thought that it would have been one of the first things she did after Silas died.

She shook her head. "No. To tell you the truth, I haven't seen much of Karen. Not for months. Silas was moping about for a while, but I didn't want to press him for details. I figured if he wanted me to know, he would tell me what was wrong. But when Karen stopped coming around, I figured they had broken up."

"Oh," was all I could manage. I took this all in. First, Karen and Silas weren't very public with their relationship. And now she hadn't been around the boardinghouse in months. But when I spoke to her, she said they were in a relationship for twenty years. Something didn't add up here, and I wasn't sure what it was.

"I better get going. I've got supper to cook for my boarders. It was nice talking to you, Rainey," she said and placed the bag of apples into her shopping cart and left.

I watched her go, not feeling right about something. Then I realized I hadn't asked her about the break-in. Not a problem. I needed an excuse to stop by and pay the boardinghouse a visit, anyway. It had been on my list of things to do for days and I hadn't gotten around to it.

Chapter Fifteen

I SPENT ANOTHER SLEEPLESS night thinking about the things I had learned about Silas's death. I still had no idea why he had been dumped in my alley. At this point I was assuming it was something random, but one thing I had come to understand about murder—most things weren't random. I had gotten to talk to Cade for a while when he got off of work, but I thought he was still keeping something from me. Not that I blamed him. He was a detective, after all, and it wasn't like he could just tell me everything he knew. He was working late hours because of the murder and I wasn't getting to see him nearly as much as I wanted to.

I picked up my nephews, Curtis and Brent from school the next day to spend some quality time with them. Which means I wanted an excuse to take them to the hobby shop and see if I could get more information out of Charlie Rhoades. With him being family to Silas, he had to know something significant about Silas's private life that I didn't yet know.

"Do they have video games in here?" Brent asked as I parked my car.

"Not really, but they do have action figures based on the characters in video games," I told him and got out of the car.

"I'd rather got to the bookstore," Curtis said, slamming the car door shut behind him.

"Maybe next time," I said while Brent hurried to the door to open it for me.

"Such a gentleman, thank you," I said as I passed through it. I didn't miss the fact that he closed the door on his brother, but I ignored it. Brothers will be brothers.

Charlie smiled big when he saw me with the boys. "Hi Rainey, I see you've brought some friends along today. What can I help you with?"

"My nephews, as promised," I said, returning his smile. "I think I'll let them have a look around and see if they can find something they want."

Curtis headed straight to the comic book rack while Brent headed to the action figures.

"Excellent," Charlie said. "If you need any help, just let me know."

"We sure will," I said, looking over some dollhouse furniture on a display next to the front counter.

"It's a lovely day," Charlie said after a few minutes of silently rearranging a display of small wooden puzzles. "Getting a little colder each day."

"It sure is," I said. "I love the fall. I can't wait for it to really get going."

"Me too," he said. His eyes went to the boys, but they were busy looking through items on the shelves. "Say Rainey, anything new on Silas's death? I'd hate for it to go unsolved."

The grin on his face told me he actually felt otherwise. "You know how it is. They've got to process evidence. How are things going down at the boardinghouse these days?"

He chuckled. "Wonderful. Nice and quiet. Everyone gets along so well lately."

"Hey, Charlie, why did you move in there? If I didn't like someone the last thing I'd want to do is move into the same house with them." He'd already told me it was because of money, but I just felt like there was something he wasn't telling me and I hoped he'd spill it.

He shrugged. "Money. I was saving every dime I had so I could open this place. Sue offers a room and two meals a day for just a bit more than the room alone. I hated working for someone else. All my life I wanted to own my own business, and while I wish I had had more starting capital when I started to invest in stock for this place, I'm pretty pleased with what I've done here."

"It is a nice little shop," I said. "We don't have anything else quite like it in Sparrow."

"That's exactly right. Plus, I'm a collector myself so it's something I have a keen interest in. That's how I funded the business. I had a few collectibles that were worth some money and as much as I hated to let them go, it was for the greater good. I figured I could buy them back as soon as I started turning a profit."

"Really? I guess it's helpful to have had a hobby that earned enough starting capital to open the shop," I said. I wasn't buying it, but he was sticking to his story. "I'm glad you had the opportunity to open this shop."

"It's the best thing I've ever done with my life."

I studied him a moment. "Charlie, can I ask you a question that might seem personal?"

He hesitated before answering. "Sure," he finally said. "Ask away."

"What happened to Silas's parents? Are they still around?" My new neighbor had already told me about Silas's parents, but I wanted to see what Charlie knew.

"His mother passed a few years ago from cancer. We don't know who his father was. Well, the official family version is that we don't know. But the truth is, I think it's Harry." He nodded with a knowing smirk.

"Harry? The grumpy guy that works at the paper?"

He nodded again. "Exactly. When I was growing up there were always whispers and some of the family wanted nothing to do with Silas. Now, I wouldn't blame them if they were going on the fact that Silas was a slimy character, but it wasn't that. It was because he was born out of wedlock and the older folk couldn't accept that."

"Really? I guess things were different years ago. That kind of thing wasn't as common and was looked down on."

"That's exactly right. Things are different these days."

"But why do you think Harry is his father?" I asked.

He shrugged. "Maybe I overheard a conversation or two." He was trying to be coy now, and it really didn't work for him.

"What was said?" I looked over my shoulder to see what the boys were doing, but they were still busily looking at comic books and action figures.

"Harry and Silas were arguing. Silas said he wanted nothing to do with Harry, then Harry said he was sorry for the trouble he had caused. At first, I thought the two had had some kind of disagreement, but then—." He stopped when two teenagers came into the shop. We waited for them to head to the comics and I turned back to him. He looked at me blankly.

"You were saying you thought at first that there was a disagreement between the two of them?"

"Oh, yes. Sorry. But then Silas said his mother deserved better, and he was sorry she ever got mixed up with him. I put it together that Harry was his father, but Silas didn't want anything to do with him."

"Do you think Harry could have killed Silas? If he was sorry for something and accepting the blame for it, I wouldn't think he planned to kill him."

"Yes, but things got ugly from there. One day Silas shoved the old man down a couple of steps and as Harry lay on the floor, Silas laughed at him and walked away. From then on, they fought terribly."

"Wow. How awful," I said. Harry was elderly and a fall like that could easily have seriously injured him.

He nodded knowingly. "I helped Harry up and made sure he wasn't hurt and he told me he would pay Silas back. He said he would make him sorry he was ever born."

"That's incredibly sad," I said. "If Harry is Silas's father, that's a whole lot of bitterness there."

"That was Silas for you. He was a cruel person. He enjoyed humiliating people. I'm not sorry he's dead. I tried to be, but I can't. It would be lying. I just hope that whoever did it, gets away with it."

I wasn't surprised that Charlie felt that way. He hadn't tried to cover up how he felt about Silas, but it made me feel a little sick, seeing a family fight that way. I didn't understand it, and I was glad that I didn't. Sometimes families paid a price just to be around one another. If Harry was capable of killing Silas, it might explain the tarp covering his body and tucked beneath him where he lay. I would think that Harry would ultimately have feelings for Silas, regardless of how he behaved toward him near the end.

"Well, I'm going to have to disagree with you on that one," I said. "I hope whoever killed Silas is caught and put away for a very long time. Whether you liked the victim or not, isn't a reason for the killer to go free."

The smile left his face. "I suppose you think I'm a monster."

"No. I don't understand you, but I don't think you're a monster."

"You might want to remember Karen and what I told you earlier about her. She needs to be checked out. If anyone had a reason to kill Silas, it was her. He strung her along for all those years and then cheated on her. She knows about it and you know that has to hurt."

"I'm sure the police are speaking to everyone that knew Silas. The killer won't get away. Not with Cade working on the case," I assured him. "Tell me, Charlie. Did you kill Silas? You have so much hatred in your heart for him."

He narrowed his eyes at me. "I did not. But I would have loved to see him suffer. Just a bit. Just so he could feel some of what he did to me."

"What did he do to you to make you hate him so much?" I asked. "I know he wrote that article, but you're carrying an awful lot of hatred in your heart for him."

He stood up straighter, his face going pink. "After he wrote that article, I got fired from my job at the bookstore. Yes, fired. I lied about being laid off. They didn't want someone working there that might have been involved in illegal activities. I tried to convince them that Silas was lying, but they wouldn't listen. Apparently Silas went to my boss and told him things about me. After that, I lost my house and my wife left me. Silas had the gall to talk to her, too. With no proof!" As he spoke, his face went from pink to a deep red and his hands gripped the edge of the counter.

"Why would your boss and your wife listen to him if he had no proof?" I asked.

"Because Silas was also having an affair with my wife. And my boss didn't like me before all this happened and this just gave him reason to fire me."

I nodded. If anyone had reason to kill Silas, it was Charlie.

Chapter Sixteen

IT WAS TWO MORE DAYS before I could get free to stop by the boardinghouse. I had begun painting the living room in my house and I hated to leave it, especially since Cade had been stopping by in the evenings to help out. I still hadn't heard back from Karen about the job, but I was hopeful. She had said she wanted me for the job and that was enough for me. Though I did wonder how awkward it might be if she were arrested for murder and I was newly hired on and dating the lead investigator.

The paint on the exterior of the boardinghouse was peeling and a window shutter on the front of the house hung slightly askew. The house had once been painted bright white, but the color had faded to a dingy gray. The shutters had faded from dark green to a dark shade of gray. Knee-high weeds chocked out the lawn and the rose bushes that once graced the front of the house were now dried up twigs. The porch ran the length of the front of the house and wrapped halfway around the side. On the side of the porch, the porch wall and railing was missing, adding to the rundown look of the place.

Karen had said the house was open and you could just walk in, so I headed up the creaking steps. The second step from the top bowed beneath my weight, startling me. Thankfully it held, and I continued on. Tentatively, I pushed open the huge front door and the smell of something old and musty hit me. I hesitated. The carpet was worn bare in spots and a small end table sat against one wall. I went to it. There was a business card holder with dust-covered cards in it. I picked one up. It had Sue's name and address on it with a line about rooms for rent. A staircase faced the foyer, and I looked up it, wondering if I should continue. Karen had said Silas's room was number six. Would that be upstairs? There were doors down the hallway, so I went toward the first one. In the middle of the door was a small brass plate with the number one on it.

I continued down the hallway. There were three rooms on each side, with number six being the last on the right-hand side. It made me wonder how many rooms this place had if there were six on the bottom floor.

I hesitated in front of the door, and glanced right and left, before taking hold of the corroded brass doorknob and giving it a turn. It stuck for a moment but then gave way. I inhaled the stale odor of the room and stepped inside, closing the door behind me.

There was a double bed with its steel frame headboard against the center of one wall. A single pillow bulged beneath a thin blue bedspread and the mattress sagged in the middle. A pair of brown leather lace-up shoes were tucked half-way beneath the bed. The closet door was open about six inches and hanging clothing could be seen through the crack. An old

Smith-Corona typewriter sat on a small wooden table and a straight back wooden chair was pushed in beneath the table.

I went to the closet and carefully pulled the sliding door open wider. Shirts and pants folded cross-wise over the hanger hung in the closet with a pair of worn and holey sneakers on the bottom of the closet. Like Cade said, Silas didn't seem to own much. That surprised me since he had lived here for so long. I moved the clothing around, hoping something of interest was tucked behind them, but I was disappointed. I slid the door closed and tried the other side of the closet, but it looked much the same as the other did.

Next, I went to the bedside table and pulled open the drawer. There was a handful of change, three pens, some business cards, and a half-empty pack of Spearmint gum. I closed the drawer. Had someone gotten to the bedroom before I had, or did Silas really not own anything of any significance? He had lived here for more than ten years and I couldn't imagine him not owning more items. Even if he didn't buy much for himself, there were birthdays, holidays, and anniversaries where others would buy presents for him. I looked around again. No laptop or computer? While Silas didn't seem to be the type that was into electronics, he had to have known how to use a computer since he worked at the newspaper.

After a quick look beneath the bed, I decided I was out of luck if I expected to find a clue to Silas's death in his room. I headed back to the door and listened a moment, then quietly pulled the door open. I nearly screamed when I saw Harry on the other side of the door.

"Hey! What are you doing in there?" he said, his bushy gray eyebrows coming together to form one long eyebrow.

"Um, I think I got lost," I said and stepped out of the room, closing the door behind me. "I really don't know my way around here, I'm afraid."

He narrowed his eyes at me. "You don't belong here. What do you want?"

"Oh, I was just stopping in to see how much it cost to rent a room here," I said. It was the first thing that popped into my head and I decided to go with it.

He seemed to consider this. "You got no business in there. Sue's gone to the market. She'll be back later and you can ask her about a room."

I nodded. "Sorry, I didn't mean to intrude. I'll certainly contact Sue about it." I really hoped to get out of there before Sue got back. I didn't want her to become suspicious of why I was here.

He stood in front of me, looking me over. "You don't look like the kind of person to live here," he said.

I wasn't sure what he meant by that, and I didn't want to ask. "It's for my father. He's on his own these days and I thought it might be nice for him since I heard Sue served meals here." My father had passed away years ago, and I hoped he didn't mind me volunteering him to live here. Not that I would do that to him, not even in his dead state would I want him to live here. This place was depressing.

He nodded slowly. "He won't want to live here. This is a bad place."

"Oh?" I asked. "What do you mean?" I didn't think he remembered me from the newspaper office, but if he did, he hadn't mentioned it.

He snorted. "Sue don't run a clean place, you can see that. She means well. Except when she's murdering people. I don't think she means well then."

I stared at him. "Murdering people?"

He nodded. "She killed Silas," he said and his voice cracked just a bit on Silas's name. "She wanted him to marry her, but he didn't want anything to do with her. She was too old for him."

"Do you really think she murdered him?" I asked.

"Of course!" he said and swayed just a little on his feet. "She has a terrible temper. There's fighting going on here all the time. Mostly it's because of Sue. She can't stay out of people's business and people get mad. Then everyone's fighting with each other." He shook his head. "No, your father is better off someplace else. Any place else."

"It seems hard for me to believe Sue could have killed someone," I said. "She seems like such a sweet woman. I work over at Sam's Diner and she comes in there sometimes." I hoped he would elaborate on the things going on here.

"Tell that to Silas. He's dead of a knife to his chest because of her," he said. "But, suit yourself. If you aren't going to worry about your father, there's nothing I can do about it. You know, you need to treat your father with more respect. He's the only one you've got and once he's gone, he's gone."

I sighed and almost agreed with him. Mine was gone, and I missed him terribly, but I was pretty sure he was speaking of Silas and himself. "I'll take your advice, then. I'll see if I can find something else for him. But, you didn't happen to see or hear anything the night Silas was killed, did you?"

"No. I was asleep. I go to bed early these days. I just can't seem to get over being tired all the time. But, when I got up the next day, Sue was mopping the kitchen floor. And if you knew Sue, you'd know there's something suspicious about that. All you could smell was pine cleaner throughout the whole house. Like she used a whole bottle."

"Sue doesn't do the floors much?"

He snorted again. "Sue doesn't do much at all. Those home-cooked meals she likes to brag on are frozen meals she heats up. You should see the kitchen. This place is a mess. Just look at it."

I glanced around me. The dust was thick on every surface and there was lint and grains of sand on the threadbare carpet. He had a point. "Well, that's very good to know before I went and rented a room for my father from her."

He hawked phlegm and nodded. "If you got any sense, you'll look elsewhere."

"I appreciate the tip," I said. He turned and staggered down the hall. Harry had been drinking. Was he just angry and bitter about Silas not accepting him as his father, or did he really know something about what happened the night Silas was killed? I wasn't sure he was in his right mind just then.

I turned to leave before Sue got back from the Market.

Chapter Seventeen

BEFORE I COULD GET to the front door, it swung open and Sue stood there, a look of surprise on her face at seeing me here. I tried to come up with something to say, but instead, I stood there, dumbly staring with my mouth open.

"Rainey," she said. A frown slipped across her face. "I didn't expect to see you here. What can I do for you?"

I forced myself to smile and stepped forward to relieve her of a couple of the bags of groceries she carried. "Let me help you with those groceries. I thought I'd stop by and see if you had a room for rent." I glanced over my shoulder at Harry, who had turned around at the appearance of Sue and was moving in closer to hear what was being said.

"Oh? I thought your mother said you just bought a house?" she asked, tilting her head. I managed to get two of the grocery bags off her arm, but she was standing there with the others still on her arm, looking at me.

"Oh, I did. It's a lovely little cottage on the other side of town. The room isn't for me. Let me help you into the kitchen with these."

She nodded, still looking confused and led the way down the hall in the direction I had just come from. "Who is the room for?" she asked looking back over her shoulder.

Did she know my father was dead? Probably so. "For my uncle. He's considering a move to Sparrow, and I was just checking out rooms and apartments. He's on a fixed income and I told him I would look around for him."

"Eh?" Harry said from behind me. He had turned again and begun following us toward the kitchen. We passed the six rooms in the hall on our way to the kitchen. "I thought you said it was for your father."

Oh Harry, go away, I thought. "Yes, this uncle has been like a father to me since my own father passed away. We're very close," I said as we entered the kitchen. It was off of the main hallway. Harry wasn't kidding about the kitchen. It needed a good cleaning. There was grease-stained wallpaper that looked to be at least from the 1950s and the stainless steel counters had smears, spills, crumbs, and a dried out half-eaten sandwich on the countertop.

"Oh, that would be so sweet to have him live so close to you then," Sue said, setting the two bags she held onto a counter. "Harry, would you be a dear and fetch the last two bags of groceries from my car?"

Harry grumbled but didn't refuse to do as she asked. His sliding footsteps echoed down the hall as he made his way to the car. I set the two grocery bags I held next to the ones she had put down.

Sue smiled again. "Now, will he want meals with his room? There's a different price for that. And if he doesn't want to buy the meals, you must tell him that under no circumstance is he allowed a hot plate in his room. He may have a small microwave and a mini-fridge, but no hotplate. Those things are dangerous."

"Do many of your boarders take their meals here?" I asked, leaning on a clean patch of the kitchen counter.

"About half of them do. The others just eat frozen meals in their rooms, mostly. Unless of course, they can't resist something I'm cooking. I'm a wonderful cook, not that I like to brag. But I can accommodate at least some of my boarders on a meal-by-meal basis. I just add it to their rent."

"That might be a good idea for my uncle. Then at least he can have a home cooked meal a couple of times a week."

She nodded. "That's what many do. But he'll have to let me know early in the day, otherwise, there's a good chance I won't have made enough. I heard you were writing another cookbook, Rainey. I know you're a good cook too, and you understand how much pride I take in my cooking."

"I do understand taking pride in your cooking. I'm hoping my new cookbook will be finished early next year," I said. I could smell stale onions as we talked, along with a slight undertone of pine cleaner.

She nodded and removed a package of shredded cheese and a gallon of milk from a shopping bag and headed to a scratched and dented commercial sized refrigerator. "You know, I've thought about writing a cookbook myself. I would hate for my family recipes to slip away with me when I'm gone. I don't have any family anymore. That's why I started the boardinghouse. My renters are like family. Most of them don't have any family of their own anymore, either." She jerked open the refrigerator door and the jars of condiments on the door-shelves rattled. She set the gallon of milk and cheese inside. "That door sticks sometimes."

"It would be a shame to allow family recipes to be lost," I agreed, wondering about what Harry said about her heating frozen food up for the residents. "Can I help you put things away?"

She waved a hand at me. "Don't worry. I've got it." She picked up a dozen eggs and two pounds of cheap margarine in stick form and headed back to the refrigerator. "Yup, I've considered doing what you're doing. I imagine if I put all my recipes into a cookbook, I'd make enough money to retire on."

I looked at her back, wide-eyed. "You might be able to make a nice little retirement income," I said, trying to be kind.

She headed back to the shopping bags. "Of course, I'm nowhere near retirement age. I've got quite a few years to go yet."

"I guess that just gives you time to write that book then," I said.

She came and stood near me, her eyes on me. "Did that detective figure out who killed Silas?"

"Not that I've heard. He's still working on it. I think these things take time, but I'm sure he'll get it sorted out soon," I assured her.

She set two wrinkled hands on the counter and was quiet a moment. "When I think of what poor Silas went through, it makes my blood boil," she said, turning to look at me.

"I don't blame you. Having a longtime friend murdered like that is heartbreaking."

She considered my words a moment. "I'll tell you something. The more I think about things, the more I think it had to be Karen Forrest that killed him."

"Why do you say that?"

"She was always so mean to poor Silas. Always ordering him around. He wanted to break up with her, but he was afraid she'd do something terrible. I can't help but think that he tried to break up with her, and she got mad and killed him. Just like he thought."

"Silas said he thought she would kill him?" I asked her.

"Well, not exactly. But he did say he was afraid of her. He was driving home one night after the two of them had a fight and a car came up behind him with its bright lights on, blinding him, and ran him off the road. He was sure it was her."

"Did he report it to the police?" I asked her.

She shook her head. "He never got a good look at the car, he was too busy trying to keep from hitting a stand of trees on the side of the road. I tell you, it had him so frightened. He confronted her, and she acted shocked and hurt." She rolled her eyes and took out a large container of oatmeal from a shopping bag.

"How frightening," I said. "That would be hard to live with. The uncertainty, I mean."

She nodded. "You better believe it," she said putting the oatmeal into a cupboard.

It was odd that Silas and Karen were together for so long without getting married, but even odder if Karen was as unstable as Sue was making her out to be. She seemed so quiet and calm. It may very well be possible that Silas stayed with her to avoid the unpleasantness of breaking up with her, but that really was a terrible way to have to live.

"Sue, were you and Silas more than friends?" I felt like I had nothing to lose by asking and I wondered what she would say.

She looked at me and her eyes went moist. "He was a gentleman. He would never cheat on Karen. But, he said if he ever got free, he would like to see where a relationship with me might lead."

"And that's why you think he tried to break it off with Karen?" I said softly.

Charlie had said he saw Sue coming out of Silas's room late at night, so I wasn't sure if she was telling me the truth about Silas not cheating on Karen. It was hard for me to think of Karen as a murderer. She was a quiet person that kept to herself and I had never seen a bit of temper, but maybe she knew how to keep it under control when others were around.

She sighed sadly. "I think so. Of course, we'll never know, will we?"

"Sue, did Silas's room get broken into recently?"

"Did someone tell you that?" she asked, eyebrows raised.

"It was a rumor I heard."

She nodded. "Yes. And I thought it was odd. He had money in his room, but they didn't take that. They took his journals. It doesn't make sense. But, I didn't think many people knew about it. He didn't want anyone to know. Who told you?"

I suddenly felt a little sick to my stomach. Karen said his journals were taken and that Silas had told Sue it was Harry that stole them. Had Karen actually stolen them to see what he was writing about her? Maybe she wanted to see if he was writing about a possible relationship with someone else? If they had had fights about Silas being interested in Sue, maybe Karen had gotten the idea that Silas was ready to break up with her so he could be with Sue and she wanted the journals for proof of it.

"Dear?" she said when I didn't answer.

"What? Oh, I'd rather not say. I hate to gossip. I shouldn't have brought it up."

She nodded. "I can guess where it came from. I suppose I should get a security system. Cameras, at the very least. Then something like that won't be able to happen without me knowing who did it."

"It might be a good idea," I said. "Can I ask you one more thing? Did you spend time in the state penitentiary?" I thought I might as well throw it out there and see where it landed.

Her face went red. "I forged a check from the grocery store I worked at. I was young. I made a mistake and I did my time. I suppose you heard that from the same source as you heard about the break-in?"

"We all make mistakes," I said. "I'm sorry, I didn't mean to upset you. Sometimes people talk and I should know better than to listen, Sue. You've been an upstanding member of the community all these years." I hoped that would smooth things over.

Harry's shuffling feet could be heard in the hallway, and she turned toward the sound.

She sighed. "That Harry. He's a difficult one. Always thinking someone is trying to make his life miserable on purpose. I suppose I should feel sorry for him, but it gets tiring."

"Here you go," Harry said, entering the kitchen. "Seems like you could do it yourself. I pay you to live here. I'm not the hired help."

"Oh, Harry, you know how I appreciate the help," Sue said good-naturedly. She turned to me and grinned.

After a few more minutes of visiting with Sue, I said my goodbyes and headed for home. Karen had some explaining to do.

Chapter Eighteen

WHAT SUE TOLD ME SURPRISED me. Did Silas really want to end his relationship with Karen? Was Karen angry about it and did she take out her anger on him? If Karen was the angry, evil person Sue made her out to be, it was possible she had killed Silas. And it made sense that she slipped into the boardinghouse to steal his journals. Even if he had kept the details of a budding relationship with Sue to himself, he would certainly pour them into those journals. I just wished I could get ahold of them. The journals would tell the tale.

I pulled into the police station and parked my car. Cade and I had a lunch date, and I hoped to get information from him about what he knew so far regarding the murder.

"Hi Buck," I said to the officer at the front desk.

"Hey, Rainey. Sam says you're making a cake. When are you going to bring it to the diner? I'd like to know in advance so I can be there for it."

I chuckled. "Soon. I promise. Can I go on back to see Cade?"

"Sure, if you promise to save me some cake," he said, one eyebrow arched. Buck was in his late forties with a head full of gray hair and a small scar on his chin, obtained while on duty years ago from a little old lady that hit him with her umbrella when he was called out to a bar on a public nuisance call. He hadn't yet lived it down.

"I tell you what. I'll make a cake just for the good officers of Sparrow and bring it down here. Then for sure, you won't miss out."

He brightened. "That's why I love you, Rainey."

I nodded. "I knew you had ulterior motives," I said and headed down the hall that led to Cade's office.

I knocked and waited.

"Come in!" he called.

I pushed the door open and smiled at him. He was sitting behind his desk, a pile of paperwork spread across the top.

"Hey," he said, smiling.

"Hey yourself. Are you ready for lunch?" My eyes went to the paperwork on his desk. "You probably should clean that desk up before you leave. Your boss might get mad." I leaned across the desk and gave him a kiss.

He chuckled. "I think it will be fine. He's come to expect this mess from me. I'll be just a minute."

I sat at a chair in front of his desk, peering at the papers scattered about. There were file folders, a copy of a speeding ticket, and a plastic bag that stuck out from beneath a file marked with Silas's name. The file was thicker than I expected and I wondered what all was in it.

"So, how's Silas's murder case coming?"

"It's coming," he said noncommittally as he squinted at the computer screen.

"Maybe it's time you got some reading glasses. You can't expect your eyes to hold out forever. Aging is a thing, you know."

He glanced at me and narrowed his eyes. "You need to keep that kind of talk to yourself. I am not aging, and neither are my eyes."

"Suit yourself. Did you find out anything about the cell phone you found in the raincoat pocket? And what about the raincoat?"

"The raincoat was made by Grubel Industries and can be purchased at a variety of different stores. Nothing special about it," he said, sitting back in his chair. "I showed it to Sue and some of the residents at the boardinghouse. Some said they thought Silas might have worn something like it, and some said they'd never seen it. The cell phone only had partial prints and the IT guy cracked it open."

"Anything interesting?" I asked, hopefully.

"It's a cheap generic throwaway phone that you need to buy a phone card for. But, there were a couple of texts, threatening the owner of the phone."

My eyes went big. "What did it say?"

"We're out of bread and milk. Pick some up at the store."

I groaned. "Tell me the truth."

"That is the truth," he said, turning to me. "The other one said 'you'll wish you hadn't.'"

"Huh. Can you trace the number it came from?" I asked. "Or was there a name mentioned in the texts?"

"They're working on it. The phone had gotten wet, so it's making it hard to recover anything else."

"I might know something," I said, teasing.

"Oh? Pray tell, what might that be?"

"Sue said Karen must have broken into Silas's room and stole the journals to find out if he was planning on breaking up with her. According to Sue, Silas was afraid of Karen and that he may have told her it was over, and Karen snapped and killed him over it. She also said Silas wanted to date her once he broke up with Karen."

He sat back in his chair and thought this over. "I suppose it's possible. With he and Karen together for so long, it would be a hard breakup. Even if they didn't have feelings for one another anymore, just the fact that they had so much history together would make it difficult to part ways. Karen would have had motive."

"Sue was in the penitentiary for forging a check from the business she worked for," I added.

"No murder in her past?"

"Nope. I want to know where those journals are," I said. "I bet they tell the tale. In detail."

"I bet they do, too. I wish someone had reported the break-in when it happened, or at the very least, when Silas turned up dead. We might have found something useful there."

"Did you find Silas's laptop or computer? He had to have had one since he was a columnist for the paper."

"He didn't have a personal computer. He used one at the newspaper. They had to force him to use it when they first began using computers years ago and he wanted nothing to do with them," he said. "By the way, I thought you were applying for a job at the newspaper?"

"I did and Karen interviewed me. She said she wanted to hire me, but she had to interview other people first and then get approval from the publisher to hire me. That doesn't surprise me about Silas. He didn't seem the type that was very tech savvy. I'm a little surprised he even had a cell phone," I said.

"We don't know that the cell phone in the raincoat was his, but Karen did say he had one. His last nod to the fact that the world was moving on," he said. "Let me get things straightened up a little and we'll go."

I smirked at him. "Your boss is okay with the mess, eh?"

"Sure. I just don't want some of these things left out," he said and began gathering papers and files together.

He moved the file on top of the clear plastic bag and there was a knife in it with dried blood on the blade. I winced.

"Silas?" I asked.

He nodded. "Sorry. I was trying to figure out where this kind of knife is sold."

The knife had a cute, decorative blade with pink and blue flowers and a bright pink handle. I had seen some knives similar to it somewhere, but I couldn't remember where. It looked to be an eight-inch chef's knife.

"That's really cute. Am I to assume it belongs to a woman?" I asked. "I wonder what Karen's kitchen knives look like?"

He shrugged. "Or it just came from a woman's kitchen. And just because it's pretty doesn't mean a woman is the killer. Maybe some rugged gentleman decided he needed a nice feminine touch in his kitchen to draw the ladies in and convince them to make him dinner?"

"Yeah, I'm sure that's it. Anything to lure a woman in."

He chuckled. "Let me get these locked up, and I'll be right back."

He left the room with the knife and the file and I sat back in my chair. His computer was still on and I debated with myself whether I should sneak a look at it before he returned and caught me at it. I couldn't hold back. I got to my feet and peered over at the computer screen. He had been searching for knife patterns. There was a Word document open beneath the Internet page and I looked over my shoulder. The door was partially open, but I didn't hear anyone in the hall. I turned back to the computer and moved the cursor to the document.

"Ah ha!" Cade said from behind me.

I jumped, slamming the mouse on the desk, and turned to face him. Heat rushed to my cheeks. "I—I."

"Yes, I know. You're nosy. Keep your hands off my computer, Rainey," he said sounding serious, and walked around to the other side of the desk and locked the computer screen.

"Sorry," I said, feeling a little foolish. "But you might try searching Walmart for knife patterns. I don't think that one is very expensive and people here in Sparrow are kind of simple folk for the most part."

"I'll take that suggestion under consult. Now, let's go get some lunch before I decide that your snooping ways aren't worth the trouble."

I snorted. He was smiling, but I knew he didn't appreciate what I had just done. I'd have to get that cake made to make it up to him.

Chapter Nineteen

I SHOWED UP AT THE newspaper to work my first day on Monday morning. Karen had called me and given me the good news on Friday and I was both nervous and excited. Sam had been hesitant when I told him about the job, worrying about whether I would still be flexible enough for the shifts I worked at the diner. But I thought it would all come together somehow. Both jobs were part-time, with the newspaper being fewer hours than the diner.

Karen met me at the door. "Good morning, Rainey. How are you?" she said brightly. She wore a business casual ensemble, and I wondered if I was under-dressed with my blouse and jeans.

"I'm excited to be here," I nearly gushed. And I was. I enjoyed writing and this job would give me a taste of something other than writing cookbooks. Maybe someday I would branch out and write other kinds of books. Maybe a novel or two.

"Let's go to my office and fill out new-hire paperwork," she said, leading the way.

Most of the other desks out front were filled, except for the one at the end. I smiled and nodded at the other staff members as I passed and got friendly reactions. That was a good start. I remembered seeing Silas sitting at the empty desk and with a sinking feeling, I realized it would probably be mine. But, no matter, I would make the best of it.

We went back into Karen's office and I took a seat. "Smells good in here," I said.

"That's my vanilla scented candle warmer. Fall makes me want to burn candles," she said. "We need to get a little paperwork filled out. I'm sure you know the drill. We need to make the government happy." She rummaged through her desk and then pulled out a file. "Just fill these out and we'll get started."

"Okay," I said, looking them over. "So, Karen, what exactly will I be doing? I know we talked briefly about it before, but how many hours a week and will I need to come into the office to do the work?"

"You'll have articles assigned to you. You'll have to come into the office at least part of the time, but I know you have another job. We can be flexible. As long as you meet the deadlines, you don't have to be tied to a set schedule. For now it will only be about ten to fifteen hours a week. We'll see how things go. It might be increased later."

I nodded and began filling out a W-2 form. "That sounds great. Sam was a little worried whether I could still make it into the diner when he needed me."

She smiled. "We're flexible. We'll work on it," she repeated.

"Will I have a chance to do other articles, besides the lifestyle ones?" I asked, looking up from the form in front of me.

"I think the chances are pretty good. Don't tell anyone, but Mary McCall is thinking about retiring. She's been here forever. The other staff will have first chance at everything, but eventually you can work your way up the ladder and get a chance to pick what you want."

"That sounds great," I said and went back to the form.

"Rainey, has Cade mentioned how the investigation is going? I keep intending to call him, but then I feel like I'd be bothering him. I know he's busy," she said, biting her lower lip. Her hands were on the desk in front of her, her fingers interlaced.

"He really is busy, but I don't think it would be a bother if you gave him a call. He doesn't go into a lot of detail with me when we talk. You know how the police are. They like to keep certain details to themselves," I said.

She nodded. "I can imagine. I just hope they find the killer soon. It would be a terrible thing if they never found his killer." She sighed and looked away.

"I wouldn't even think about it. I know Cade well enough to know he won't give up on it. Have you heard anything new? Or maybe remembered something that might be of help in solving the crime?"

She looked at me again and shrugged. "I keep racking my brain, trying to come up with something I overlooked, but I can't think of a thing. I've hardly slept since it happened. I hope he didn't suffer," she said, her voice cracking. "I can't stand knowing his killer is on the loose. What if they kill again?"

"I know what you mean. I feel exactly the same way. I'm thankful Cade is on the case though. He really is dedicated to finding Silas's killer."

"I know, I shouldn't worry," she said, sitting back in her chair.

I turned back to my forms, but then looked at her again. "Karen, if you don't mind me asking, how was your relationship with Silas?"

Her brows flew up. "Why do you ask that?"

"I don't know. You two were together for so long. Sometimes relationships grow stale."

She narrowed her eyes at me. "Our relationship was fine. We were happy. When you're together for a long time, you know so much about one another and you don't need that crazy, exciting romance you had in the early days of the relationship. You learn what's important and you know those earlier feelings don't last forever. Why are you asking?"

I swallowed. "So, Silas had no plans of breaking up with you?" I decided to be upfront. I wanted to see her reaction and hear her answer.

Her breath caught, and she was quiet. I could see tears welling up in her eyes. "Of course not! We were happy!" she said suddenly. "We just celebrated our twentieth anniversary. Where is this coming from, Rainey?"

"Nowhere, Karen," I said gently. "I'm sorry. I didn't mean to upset you. I'm just as stumped as everyone else as to who would want to kill Silas."

"Well, it wasn't me!" Karen nearly shouted. She stopped and pulled herself together. "I'm sorry. I'm not usually an emotional person, but this thing has me shook. You can understand that, can't you?"

I nodded. "I certainly do understand. I'm sorry. For everything. I didn't mean to upset you."

She nodded, accepting my apology. "I know Cade will figure this thing out. He has to. But I will tell you this. The more I go over things, the more I think Harry may have had a hand in this. He called in sick the night Silas was killed and the two of them couldn't get along. I asked Silas once why he didn't help Harry and give him a ride to the newspaper—Harry doesn't own a car. Silas got angry and said he didn't owe that old man anything. There was just something between the two of them."

I wondered if she knew that Harry was Silas's father. If she did, she wasn't volunteering that information. "But Harry's pretty elderly. He doesn't move very quickly and I would think that in order to stab someone in the chest, you'd have to have some strength and be able to move quickly in case the victim fought back."

"I know he's elderly, but he's stronger than you think. Being the janitor here, he does some work around here that takes a lot of strength. I've seen him lift boxes of supplies that are heavy. And if Silas was asleep when he stabbed him, it wouldn't have been difficult for him to kill him."

She had a point. The killer may have slipped into Silas's room while he slept that night and stabbed him. Cold blooded. Silas wouldn't have had a chance to fight back or alert anyone that there was a killer in the boardinghouse. If he was killed there, that is.

"I suppose it's possible," I said.

"It is possible. Especially if he had help getting the body out of the boardinghouse. Silas was so thin. He hardly weighed 120 pounds. Harry might not have needed any help at all."

"He was that thin?" I asked. I knew Silas was thin, but I hadn't realized he weighed that little.

She nodded. "He ate like a horse, but he had a fast metabolism. He never put on weight. It wouldn't have taken an extremely strong person to drag him to a vehicle and dump his body in your alley."

"That's something to consider," I said, sitting back in my seat.

And it was. I still had trouble believing Harry could do such a thing. He reminded me of someone's grandpa and I wanted to believe he didn't have it in him to murder someone while they slept. But, if Harry slipped into Silas's room late at night while he slept, he could have easily stabbed him. Most of the people at the boardinghouse were elderly, and some didn't hear well. The more I thought about it, I realized the porch at the boardinghouse was just about the right height to transfer a body from it to the bed of a pickup, and a pickup has larger tires, just like the tracks made in the mud in my alley. If Harry had an accomplice with a pickup, it was a definite possibility.

Chapter Twenty

"GUESS WHAT TOMORROW is?" Mom asked. We were getting a coffee at Agatha's and I was keeping one eye on the clock. I needed to stop in and put some time in at the newspaper today. I had been given an assignment, and I was excited to get it completed before my deadline.

"I don't know. What day is tomorrow?" I said and took a sip of my latte. I was getting as much pumpkin spice in as I could while it was here.

"The day before your birthday party. We need that cake done. What flavor did you settle on?" she asked, leaning back in her chair.

"What do you mean tomorrow is the day before my birthday party? My birthday isn't until next Wednesday."

"Yes, but Saturday is the closest weekend day to your birthday without going over. We're having it Saturday at seven."

"What difference does it make if it goes over? Why don't we just have a little get-together Wednesday night for cake and ice cream? We don't need to invite that many people. Just Agatha, Cade, some people from the diner, and then a few people that Stormy wants."

I was still tying to figure out how to keep from having to invite Georgia. She couldn't stand me, but I thought if I invited everyone else from the diner, I had to invite her. I doubted she would attend, but I was worried she would spoil things if she decided to come. She might come just for spite.

"We're having dinner. I'm having Tony's Tacos cater it and then we'll have the cake."

I sighed. I didn't want my birthday to be blown out of proportion, but with Mom at the helm, there was no other way for it to go. "Okay, then. How many people? And where are we having it?"

"About sixty. We're having it at the boardinghouse." She took a deep drag on the straw stuck into her iced coffee without looking at me.

"Wait. What? What do you mean we're having it at the boardinghouse? Why on earth are we having it there?"

"Because Sue offered. She has a large dining room, and it's free," she said. "It will save me money and there won't be much clean up. Sue offered to handle it."

"Mom, I don't mean to be rude, but that place isn't the cleanest place around. Why don't we just have a smaller get-together at your house? Or my house," I said, feeling alarmed. It was nice of Sue to offer, but I really didn't want to have it there.

"Relax. The food will be brought in. It's not like we'll be cooking it there. She's been so down since her friend Silas died. She offered the place and I couldn't say no. I thought it would cheer her up, and you know what? It did. You should have seen the smile on her face when I said yes." Mom patted my hand like she had it all taken care of.

I couldn't believe I was hearing this. "Please, Mom. Not there. I don't feel comfortable about it." I didn't want to tell her that Silas might have been murdered there.

"I know it's important for you to help others, Rainey. And Sue needs our help to pull her out of the doldrums. Stormy already said it was fine."

I sighed. "I hope you're right."

There was no way I was going to allow this dinner to be held at the boardinghouse. I'd find another place to hold it, and then convince Stormy to tell Mom she needed to change the venue. There was no use in arguing with her right now.

"How's the new job going?" she asked, changing the subject.

"It's fine. I'm writing an article on the new furniture store that opened up last month. I saw some cute items at the store and I need to get a few things for my house," I said.

She nodded. "That's nice dear. I'm glad you got another job," she said and looked over her shoulder. "I need to talk to Agatha. I'll be right back."

She got up and headed to the front counter. I took a sip of my latte and spied Harry across the room at a corner table. I got up and headed over to him.

"Hi, Harry," I said. "How are you this afternoon?"

He slowly looked up at me and grunted.

"Mind if I sit?" I asked.

He considered this a moment, then shrugged. "Suit yourself."

I took a seat across from him and set my latte down. "Sure is a nice day out, isn't it?"

He looked at me suspiciously. "I suppose. If you like that sort of thing."

"So, we're coworkers now. That's exciting," I said.

"Coworkers? So are you going to be cleaning toilets with me?" he asked, peering at me over his glasses.

"Um no, not exactly. I'm going to be writing articles for the newspaper," I explained.

"I guess we aren't coworkers then, are we?" he said with a snort. "Darned writers. All they do is sit around at their desk and gossip."

I stared at him a few moments. "Oh. Well. I guess I'll have to work on that, then. The not sitting around and gossiping part."

"Suit yourself," he repeated and shrugged again. He folded over the newspaper and then took a drink of his coffee. There was no lid, and he took his coffee black. Somehow I thought that was the way someone like him would drink it. Nothing fancy.

"So, I hear there will be some excitement at the boardinghouse this weekend." I waited, but Harry didn't look up. "I hear there will be some excitement at the boardinghouse this weekend," I repeated.

"I heard you. I just don't care," he said finally looking up.

"Oh. Well, in that case, let me tell you. We're having a birthday party and I'm making a cake. I think I'm making a vanilla layer, a white chocolate raspberry layer, and a lemon layer. Doesn't that sound good, Harry?" I asked him, trying to sound excited.

"I like chocolate. And not that white chocolate stuff. That isn't real chocolate," he said looking at me.

"Sorry. I don't think we'll have chocolate this time. It's a shame Silas won't be there to join in the festivities."

"It's a good thing he isn't. He'd get drunk and ruin the whole thing."

"Really? I didn't know he drank," I said and took a sip of my coffee.

"Do you live under a rock? Silas was always causing trouble when he drank. I bet he was arrested so many times he lost count."

I smiled. "I guess I must live under a rock then," I said. "It was kind of Sue to allow us to use the boardinghouse."

"It's a filthy mess. I hope you intend to stop by early and clean it."

"I just might do that," I said. With baking the cake, it would be a tight squeeze time-wise, but it was a good idea if I couldn't find another place to hold the party. I could do it under the guise of decorating and Stormy and Mom and I could at least clean up the dining room.

"She did it, you know. I told you that. Her and that Karen. They got together and killed him," he suddenly said, leaning toward me and whispering.

"They did it together? Why didn't you mention that the other day? You said it was Sue by herself." I wasn't sure I believed Harry. It seemed like he might be imagining things because I couldn't see Sue and Karen getting together to do anything.

"I was thinking about it. They had to do it together. Mark my words. They did it."

I nodded. "I'm certainly going to look into it," I said, hoping to appease him.

"How else would Sue have gotten his body out of the house? She needed help. She killed Silas. You look into that and let me know what you find out. I know you're asking all these questions because you're helping that detective. Now, I've got work to do." He stood to his feet, picked up his paper and coffee, and headed toward the door.

I sighed. I needed to be more careful in how I spoke to people if it was that obvious I was trying to find the killer.

Silas being as thin as he was wouldn't have been difficult to move. But, dead weight was dead weight.

Chapter Twenty-one

"YOU KNOW WHAT I THINK we should do?" Cade asked me.

"No, what?" I said.

"Go camping down at the river before the weather turns too cold," he said and grabbed me around the waist, pulling me to him as I walked by. "We can go fishing."

I giggled as he kissed me. "It already *is* too late. Haven't you been outside in the early morning? It's freezing!" Fall was settling in and as much I liked to go camping once in a while, it was far too cold to be sleeping in a tent this time of year.

"Don't be a baby. It's not that cold," he teased.

"It's far too cold. We should have done it over the summer when it was hot. Now let me go so I can get the cake put together."

Sue had suddenly canceled on my mother and we were forced to move the party to the reception hall of the local wedding chapel. I wasn't sad about it. It was less work for me since I didn't have to clean the boardinghouse dining room.

Cade and I were the first to arrive at the hall, and after carefully maneuvering each cake layer into a box and then transporting them in the back of Cade's car, I was about to put it together. It resembled a medium-sized wedding cake and was probably far too big for the get-together, but I didn't care. I had enjoyed baking and decorating it. The top and bottom layers had rolled fondant icing and Stormy's middle layer had buttercream frosting with extra vanilla. At first I didn't think it would look right with both types of frosting, but in the end, I liked it. It gave the cake depth and texture.

Cade kissed me again and released me. "I'll get the rest of the things from the car."

"You do that," I said with a chuckle.

When I had the cake together and sitting on a stand, I began moving the tables so that they formed a 'U' shape. I wanted everyone to be able to look at one another and I wanted the cake to sit on the center table. It was beautiful, if I did say so myself.

"Hey, can I help?" Sam asked, walking through the door. He had two pink striped gift bags, one in each hand.

"Sam, I hope those aren't what I think they are. I told you, no gifts."

"I don't care. I wanted to get you and Stormy a little something, so I did. Besides, I'm getting tacos and some delicious cake. It's the least I could do."

"You're so sweet," I said and gave him a peck on the cheek. Sam really was the best boss anyone could ask for. "Why don't you put them on that table in the corner and then help me move these other tables into a 'U' configuration."

"I like it," he said and put the gift bags where I had pointed and then went to the end of one of the tables that I needed to move. "That way everyone has to participate in socializing."

"It's a diabolical plan, but I had to do it," I said. "No wallflowers at my party."

"Hey Sam," Cade said, returning with a bag of plates, plastic ware, and other party items.

"Hey Cade. Any news on Silas's killer yet?" he asked.

"We're working on it. I've interrogated half the town. I'm sure someone will break under the pressure any day now," Cade said.

"That's what I like to hear. Do whatever it takes to get them to confess," Sam said with a chuckle.

"You two are terrible," I said and stepped back to let them finish moving the table as Cade sidled up to my end and picked it up.

"I WANT CAKE, PLEASE," Lizzy said. Her cute little nose was smudged with guacamole and she gave me her best smile, trying to convince me to let her have cake now.

"Soon, Lizzy. I promise. We'll have cake very soon."

The party was in full swing and thankfully, there weren't nearly as many people here as Mom had threatened to invite. A quick guess said there were probably a little over thirty. I saw Sue in a corner talking to Karen and it made the hair on the back of my neck stand up. I had thought they weren't friends. According to Charlie Rhoades, they had fought on the front porch. Loudly. I watched them for several minutes, and then I searched for Cade. He was being cornered by my mother. If I could get around the people and the tables, I would point out Sue and Karen to him. Those two were up to something.

I saw Stormy on the other side of the room, and I hoped she was holding up. Not having Natalie here was hard for her and I hoped she at least got to talk to her earlier. We had been so busy since the party began that I hadn't gotten a chance to ask.

"Can we have cake? Bonney asked, tugging on my dress. Bonney was Stormy's middle daughter, and she was as cute as her sisters were.

"Sure honey, in a few minutes," I promised and kept making my way toward Cade.

"Stormy!" Gail Simpson said, catching me by the hand. "Happy birthday!"

"Thanks so much, but it's Rainey," I said, smiling. Gail was my mother's neighbor, and she had already wished me happy birthday three times. I could never figure how some people instantly knew which one of us was which, while some never got it right.

She blushed. "Oh, there I go again. Well, something tells me someone wants you to have an especially happy birthday since I can't seem to stop telling you that."

"Well, I do appreciate it," I said with a smile. "Stormy's over there." I pointed her out. Stormy was wearing a lavender colored dress while I had gone with red. I would have thought she would have at least noticed that much.

"Hi Rainey," a voice said, and I turned around to see Sue standing there. She had worn a navy blue and white striped knit dress that was stretched out at the neck. "Happy birthday! I've been trying to get over to talk to you all evening."

"Thanks Sue, I'm glad you made it," I said, and glanced at Cade. I hoped he had a chance to see Sue and Karen huddled together in the corner before they split up.

"Can we talk in private?" she whispered.

"Um, sure we can do that," I said. I wondered what she needed to talk to me about. I was bummed that I hadn't gotten to Cade in time.

She led the way out the door and I followed her down the hall to the bathroom. Once inside, she looked beneath the stall doors.

"We're alone," she whispered. "I'm so sorry I had to cancel your using the boardinghouse. I hated to do it, but my refrigerator went out on me and there wouldn't be any place to keep the ice cream and punch."

"That's no problem. It's completely understandable," I said, wondering why she needed to bring me in here to tell me that.

"I wanted to tell you that I think you need to come back to the boardinghouse tomorrow and take a look at something I found."

"Oh?" I asked. "What is it?"

She put one hand on her throat and looked around the empty bathroom. "Harry killed Silas. I don't want to alarm anyone, but it's important that you come by tomorrow."

I studied her. She had already told me she suspected Harry, and then she said she thought Karen was the killer. Why had she gone back to her first suspicion? And why did she think it was important for me to stop by? Cade had said he had already looked the place over and didn't find much.

"Why? What did you find?" I asked, trying to keep the building annoyance out of my voice.

"A stain on the floor of the men's bathroom. It looks like dried blood."

"How come you're just now noticing it?" I asked. It had been several weeks since Silas had been killed and it seemed like the floor should have been mopped several times by now.

"Oh, I usually let the men take care of cleaning up in there. You know how men can be. Anyway, I had a feeling it wasn't being done, so I went in there. There's a throw rug in there and when I moved it, I saw a stain. It looked like dried blood." She nodded.

"Maybe we should talk to Cade, then. He'll want to see it and take a sample from it," I said.

She shook her head. "Can you just stop by tomorrow and take a look at it? I'd hate to have made a mistake and have it be nothing but dried rust. I'd feel foolish."

"But if Harry really did kill Silas, doesn't it worry you to be under the same roof with him?"

"No, I installed new locks on all the doors and I've instructed all of my boarders to keep their doors locked. Everyone has been worried since Silas was killed. You know how older folk can be. I know they're keeping the doors locked. Besides, it's not like Harry has a reason to hurt anyone else. It was Silas he had a problem with. Since he's been gone, Harry has been happy as a clam."

"Really? Happy?" I said. He hadn't been especially happy when I talked to him two days earlier.

She nodded. "He's been singing in the mornings. He's sure happy about something."

I nodded. "I'll stop by first thing in the morning."

"Let's keep this to ourselves, shall we? Until you get a look at it?"

"Sure," I said. I was lying. I was going to let Cade know and maybe he'd come along. I'd make something up to tell her tomorrow when he showed up with me. I didn't like that she had huddled in the corner with Karen after accusing her of killing Silas and I wasn't taking any chances.

Chapter Twenty-two

CADE WAS UNABLE TO stop by the boardinghouse with me the following day. He had some meetings with his boss and a visiting dignitary that he couldn't get out of, but he had promised he would stop by after lunch. I had to work the lunch shift at the diner so that meant I wouldn't be able to go with him. The idea of a great discovery at the boardinghouse, no matter how slight a chance it was, was just too much for me. I wasn't going to wait, nor would I let Cade go there without me when I had been invited to see what was there.

As luck would have it, I couldn't make it early in the morning like I had planned due to a pipe beneath my kitchen sink bursting in the early morning hours. By the time the plumber had stopped by and given his assessment, it was nearly time for my shift at the diner. No matter. I would stop at the boardinghouse before work. By the time I had dealt with the water pipe, I had convinced myself the stain was nothing, anyway.

"Hi, Sue," I said when I walked into the boardinghouse. She had a blue feather duster and was working on removing the coat of dust on the spindles on the staircase. So much for Harry's opinion that she didn't clean. She may not have been good at it, but clearly, she tried.

"Hi, Rainey, how are you?" she asked, beaming. "I was beginning to worry about you. I thought you'd be by earlier."

"I'm sorry, I had a busted pipe beneath my kitchen sink that I had to take care of. I've got to be at the diner in half an hour, but I thought I'd stop by before I went."

She nodded. "I'm so glad you did. Follow me," she said.

I followed her down the hall and we stopped at the door marked 'men'. She looked both ways and then knocked softly. When no one answered, she knocked again, this time a little louder. There was still no answer, so she turned the doorknob and pushed the door open.

We walked into the bathroom, and I glanced over my shoulder to make sure no one saw us. Sue closed the door behind us and locked it. The yellow linoleum on the floor had cracks and splits in it and someone had tried to repair the seam where two pieces met with duct tape that was now curling up. There was a rust ring around the drain on the sink but the lid to the toilet was thankfully closed.

She pushed aside a throw rug in the middle of the floor with her foot and beneath it was a dark stain that looked more like rust than anything else. I squatted and looked at it. I wasn't going to touch it, but I wanted a better look. It seemed that it had probably been there for some time, dark in the center and lighter on the edges. But the more I looked at it, the more I thought it couldn't be rust. The lighter edges would have been more orange. It may not have been rust, but I really didn't think it was dried blood.

"What do you think?" she asked, squatting easily across from me.

I was surprised by her agility. At her age, I would have thought she would have moved stiffly and that her knees would have creaked.

"I don't think it looks like blood."

"You don't?" she said, sounding disappointed. "Well, what is it?"

I shrugged. "I have no idea."

"Well, shouldn't the police take a sample and send it to the lab? That's what they do, don't they?" she asked.

"They do. Did Cade come in here when he stopped by after the murder?"

She nodded "Yes, but the rug was covering it. I wouldn't have seen it myself, but I was going to take up the rug to wash it. He probably missed it."

"It's possible," I said. I hated to tell her I thought it was a waste of time for Cade to stop by, but it most likely would be. Cade would have done a thorough job inspecting the place the first time, unless he really hadn't suspected that Silas had been murdered here. "I think Cade would have already seen it." He hadn't mentioned it when I told him about it the night before, but this really didn't look like anything important anyway.

"Perhaps. So do you think I shouldn't waste his time?" she asked.

"I think he should be made aware of anything that looks suspicious. It won't hurt to let him know. I'll call him on my way to the diner and tell him about it. He may be able to stop by this afternoon." I didn't want to let her know that Cade was in fact already planning on stopping by since she hadn't wanted me to tell him in the first place.

She nodded and stood up easily. "That sounds good."

I straightened up and pulled my cell phone from my pocket and sent him a quick text so Sue would know I had sent it. "There. I sent him a text instead of calling. I think he'll stop by," I said.

She nodded. "Rainey, would you like to have a quick bite of the cinnamon crumb cake I baked? I know you're an excellent baker and cook and I feel like something's missing. I know you said you were on your way to work, but would you mind? It'll only take a minute."

I hesitated, remembering what Harry had said about her not keeping a clean house. Surely she would make sure the food she made was handled hygienically. "Sure," I said, deciding to take a chance.

"Thanks so much," she said, and I followed her out of the bathroom and into the kitchen.

The kitchen smelled faintly of cinnamon and she removed the lid from an aluminum pan, revealing the cake. The crumbled topping was slightly burned, and I steeled myself, wishing I hadn't agreed to try it.

"It smells good," I said. And it did at least smell good beneath the slightly burned scent of the topping.

There was a knock on the kitchen doorframe and we both turned to look. Karen stood, one hand raised from knocking. We both stared at each other. From what I had been told by Charlie, she and Sue hated each other, and yet they had huddled together in a corner last night, whispering. And now here she was. She smiled.

"Hi, Rainey. Sue," she said and nodded.

"Hi, Karen. Fancy meeting you here," I said.

"I was going to say the same about you," she said with a chuckle. "I just stopped by to pick up some of Silas's things." Her eyes went to Sue, and she smiled at her.

"Oh," I said, and I glanced at Sue.

"I'll get those for you," Sue said. "I was just going to have Rainey take a bite of my cinnamon crumb cake. Something doesn't seem quite right and I just know she'll know what to do about it."

"Well if anyone would know, it would be Rainey," Karen agreed. "It does smell delicious."

"But perhaps a bit overdone," Sue said, eyeing the cake in the pan. "Why don't you come in and sit at the kitchen table and have a bite? Maybe you can weigh in with your opinion."

"That does sound lovely," Karen said, walking all the way into the kitchen. Her eyes went to me, and if I wasn't mistaken, she seemed a little nervous.

Sue went to the cupboard and took down some plates. Then she got out a cake cutter from a drawer and brought them to the table. I picked up the cake pan and brought that to the table for her.

We sat around the small wooden kitchen table and Sue handed plates around. "I don't know about the two of you, but I love fall and cinnamon is the iconic scent of fall."

"Me too," I said, keeping an eye on Karen. "It's my favorite time of year."

"You can say that again," Karen said, nodding. Her eyes went to Sue and then back to me.

Sue put the tip of the cake server into the center of the cake, and the cake began to crumble beneath it, making an uneven cut. "Oh dear. I think I should get a knife. I may have left the cake in the oven for far too long." She laughed and got up, heading to the kitchen counter. "I'm sorry if it is overdone."

"I think it will be fine," I said, peering at the cake again. I had a feeling it would be extremely dry, but I didn't want to hurt her feelings.

Sue opened another drawer and pulled out a knife and returned to the table. "There now, this should do it."

My eyes went to the knife, and it was all I could do to keep from gasping. The blade of the knife had a pink and blue floral pattern.

Chapter Twenty-three

I LOOKED AT KAREN, but she didn't seem to notice the knife. Harry was right. The two of them killed Silas. I swallowed as Sue looked at me.

"Are you all right, Rainey? Are you feeling sickly?" she asked, frowning. "You suddenly look a bit pale."

"What?" I said, trying to keep my wits about me. "No, not at all. I'm fine. I just can't wait to have a taste of that cake." I forced myself to smile.

She smiled and began cutting the cake with the knife. I glanced at Karen. She was watching me. That was when I realized Sue and Karen had lured me here to kill me. I had been asking too many questions. Even Harry had noticed. Karen and Sue had gathered together in the corner the night before, plotting how they could get me over here. That spot in the bathroom looked nothing like blood, and Sue knew it.

The kitchen was large, and the doorway was all the way on the other side of the room. I could make a run for it, but Sue was in my path to the door and I wanted to make sure I had a good shot at getting out of here before I made a try for it.

"That does look good," Karen said as Sue handed her a piece of cake. Sue had swirled cinnamon throughout the cake and it probably would be tasty if it hadn't been over-cooked. As it was, it crumbled dryly.

"Here you are, Rainey," Sue said, handing me a plate with a piece of cake on it.

"Thanks, Sue. Smells great," I said taking the plate and setting it down in front of myself. Then I realized the cake might be poisoned. I looked at Karen. She hadn't taken a bite of her own cake yet. "Doesn't it smell good, Karen?" I wanted to see if she would taste hers before I tasted mine. If it was poisoned, there was no way she was going to do that.

She looked at me. "It does smell delicious." She made no move to take a bite, so I turned to Sue.

"What do you think, Sue?" I asked, hoping she would take a bite.

"I think I want to leave the critique to the professional. Please, take a bite."

I looked at the cake in front of me.

"What's wrong, Rainey?" Sue asked when I just sat and stared at it.

My eyes went to the knife lying beside the cake pan. It was the same exact pattern as the knife that killed Silas. Harry could have come to the kitchen to get the knife to kill Silas, but I doubted it. It was these two. Sue and Karen killed Silas. It made perfect sense.

I couldn't take my eyes off of the knife. "I'm sorry. I suddenly do feel a little unwell. I had a migraine earlier and sometimes the nausea sticks around even after the headache is gone." I forced myself to look at her and I gave her a weak smile.

Her eyes went to the knife, and she slowly looked at me, understanding dawning on her about what I knew. She forced herself to smile, and she looked at Karen. "Karen? What do you think?"

Karen looked at me funny, then took a small bite of the cake. "Mm, it's good," she said. "Very cinnamony."

"Not too dry?" Sue asked her, but looking at me again.

"Well, maybe a bit. But it's still very tasty," Karen said. "Rainey, I'm sorry you don't feel well. Maybe the cake will help settle your stomach. When I get nauseous, I eat crackers or dry toast. It helps a lot."

"Thanks," I said weakly.

Sue took a bite of her cake. "That is dry. I guess I should have kept a closer eye on it. That's a shame, but I guess I'll know for next time."

I looked from one to the other and then sat back in my chair, suddenly feeling foolish. What was I thinking? I watched as they both took a bigger bite of their cake. My imagination was running away with me.

I felt terrible about what I had been thinking about them, so I picked up my fork and took a bite of the cake. It was very dry but otherwise had a good flavor. "It's not bad, Sue," I said. "It is a little overdone, but you did a really good job."

She brightened. "Why, thank you, Rainey. That means a lot coming from you."

I smiled and took another bite.

"Oh, I better get that box of Silas's things for you, Karen," Sue said and got up from the table.

While Sue was gone, Karen and I made small talk, my eye going to the knife again. If I could get it, Cade could run it through forensics or whatever it was he did with things like that to see if it was an exact match. I was sure it was. But with Karen at the table I couldn't risk taking it. I wasn't completely sure she wasn't involved in Silas's murder. I would text Cade and let him know as soon as I got out of here.

"Here we are," Sue said, bringing a small box to the table.

"Thank you so much, Sue," Karen said, getting to her feet. She hadn't finished her cake, and I looked at it, wondering. "I've got to get back to the newspaper now. I appreciate this."

"It's no problem," Sue said pleasantly. "I guess these things should go to you. You were with him for so long."

Sue looked sad, and I wanted to feel sorry for her, but I didn't know if I should.

"I think I better get going, too. I've got to get to the diner," I said, standing up.

"Oh, Rainey, will you wait a moment? I want to get you the recipe for the cake. Maybe you can make suggestions on how to improve it?"

I hesitated. I wanted out of this place. "Sure," I said instead.

Karen said her goodbyes and left. When she was out of the house, Sue picked up the knife. "I hate to do this to you, Rainey. But I know you know. I have no choice."

Chapter Twenty-four

"I DON'T KNOW WHAT YOU'RE talking about," I said, looking at the knife in her hand. "That's a lovely knife. I was just admiring it. I need a new knife set for my new house."

"Stop it. Do you think I'm that stupid? I know that you know." Sue glared at me, her mouth forming a hard line.

I shook my head. "Listen, Sue, I've got to get to work. I appreciate the cake and I'll definitely talk to Cade about the stain in the bathroom. It doesn't really look like blood, but it's good for him to check it out. In fact, Cade said he thought Silas was killed somewhere else. The alley, I think was what he said."

"You know I killed Silas. Don't play stupid with me. I didn't want to. I had to do it. And now I have to kill you. If you weren't so nosy, asking all over town about Silas's murder, I could sit here, home free. But no. You had to get involved. Well, I'm not going to jail just because you can't mind your own business."

"I don't believe you killed him," I said, still hoping for an out. If I could get in a position to knock that knife out of her hand, I could get free. "I know Cade is looking at Harry." I had no idea who Cade was looking at, but if it worked to distract her, then I would use it.

She looked a little uncertain, and then her mouth formed a hard line again. "I killed Silas. I didn't want to do it, but I had no choice. He was two-timing me with Karen. He said he would break it off with her, but he didn't."

"I don't blame you for being angry, then. No one deserves to be cheated on. But, he was seeing Karen for so long. It shouldn't have been a surprise that he couldn't break it off," I pointed out.

She narrowed her eyes at me. I realized I had probably taken the wrong approach with her in pointing out that he would have trouble breaking up with Karen.

"He belonged with me!" she shouted.

"Was it worth killing him over?" I asked, slowly getting to my feet. I wondered if anyone else was in the boardinghouse. I might need some backup and I hoped there was someone spryer than Harry around.

"I asked him to marry me. He just laughed at me. Can you believe that? He laughed at me!"

I heard a creak from the floor in the hall, but Sue didn't turn around. "Why would he do that?" I asked, hoping to keep her talking. "He seemed like a nice guy."

She snorted. "He was a cheating liar. He promised to break it off with Karen. He said he didn't love her like he loved me. I gave him discounts on rent, and I gave him free meals. He used me!"

Karen peeped around the corner of the kitchen doorway and put a finger to her lips. I tried to keep from looking at her.

"That's terrible," I said, keeping my eyes on Sue. "Some people have no ethics. I'm sorry he treated you that way. I wish you had talked to someone before it came to murder though.

Maybe we can talk to Cade and see if there's a solution to your predicament." It was a long shot that she would buy this, but I wanted to give Karen time to get closer to Sue. She was now tiptoeing very slowly behind her.

"I—I don't think there's a solution at this point. Is there? I mean, Silas is dead, after all," she said, softening. "I just wish he had listened to reason. That man never did. He was always so hardheaded. I tried and tried to get him to understand he was better off with me. He already lived here. How much easier would it have been for him to just marry me?"

"Some people are like that," I said as Karen reached around from behind Sue and hit the hand she held the knife in.

Sue became startled and screamed as the knife flew from her hand, clattering on the linoleum beneath the table. I scrambled and grabbed it while Karen wrapped her arms around a struggling Sue.

"You stop that!" Sue screamed and tried to break free of Karen's grip. "Let go of me! I'll kill you, Karen!"

"Silas loved me!" Karen insisted, holding on to Sue as tightly as she could. "You were nothing to him!"

I pulled my phone out of my pocket and called Cade. He was never going to believe this one.

"Stop it!" Sue cried. "Silas said he couldn't stand you! Silas loved me! He loved me!"

"You fool! If he loved either of us, he never would have cheated," Karen grunted as she held Sue's arms tightly.

Truer words were never spoken.

Chapter Twenty-five

I LEANED AGAINST CADE, and stared into the fire. It was the first fire I had built in my fireplace in my new house. Actually, Cade built it, but it didn't matter. The weather had turned chilly and it was warm and comforting. The light from the fire illuminated the living room and we each had a cup of cocoa, complete with floating marshmallows on top.

"What happened with Sue when you got her to the station?" I asked after staring at the fire and feeling myself begin to nod off.

He chuckled quietly. "Kind of a sad case, really. She loved him. But when he laughed at her proposal, she had finally had enough of his refusing to lover her back, and she stabbed him. She said she didn't know why she did it. She just went into a rage and it was over before she knew it."

I nodded. "Why was he in my alley?"

"It was a random choice. She managed to drag him out onto the front porch of the boardinghouse, then into the back of Silas's pickup."

"That porch is just about the height of a pickup bed, isn't it?" I said.

He nodded. "Made it easy on her. It also helped that Silas was so skinny. He couldn't have weighed much."

I shook my head. "What a waste. No one is worth murdering. It's not like she gets to be with him now. One life snuffed out and another ended by what will be a long jail sentence."

"The love lives of some people are complicated," he said and took a sip of his cocoa. "Not like mine, of course."

"You can say that again. It's not like she was going to get away with it with you on the case, and at her age, she'll never see freedom again."

He chuckled. "And with you on the case. You're a nosy one, have I ever told you that?"

I giggled. "You may have mentioned that in the past. It's what I'm good at, and I figure I should do what I'm good at. Sue said she gave Silas discounts on the rent and free food. He was playing her and probably never had any feelings for her."

"I don't know why Sue bothered with the proposal in the first place. She was the one that made it look like someone broke into his room. She stole his journal, read it, and knew he was still in love with Karen. She admitted she wanted to scare him, and find out how he really felt about her when she broke into his room. Turned out he never even mentioned her in the journals and that made her angrier."

I sighed. "Maybe she wanted to give him one last chance before she killed him and hoped he may have written that he loved her in the journals. I don't understand some people. If you ever decide you want to see someone else, then do it. But know that I am not going to kill anyone to win you back or to get revenge."

"What? I'm not worthy of such passion? I'm hurt."

"You'll have to be hurt then. You aren't worth murdering. Seriously, let me know if you want to be with someone else." I took a sip of my cocoa.

He snickered. "Just like that? It's over if some cute girl crosses my path and I take a liking to her?"

"Yup."

He pulled me closer and kissed me, then looked me in the eye. "I don't intend to hurt you. Let the past go."

Tears sprang to my eyes. It seemed like he knew me better than I knew myself. I nodded. "Okay." All men weren't like my ex-husband. I needed to keep that thought at the forefront of my mind or I was going to destroy this relationship.

We spent the rest of the evening together, not saying much. We didn't need to. We were happy. I felt bad for both Karen and Sue. Silas wasn't worth the effort. If he couldn't decide which woman he really wanted to be with, they both should have walked away. Playing both was a deadly game.

The End

Sneak Peek

HOT CIDER AND A MURDER

A Rainey Daye Cozy Mystery, book 6

Chapter One

"My cider punch is going to knock 'em dead tonight," I said to Cade as I poured the cranberry juice into the crockpot.

Cade leaned over my shoulder, watching what I was doing. "Cranberry juice? I thought you said you were making hot apple cider?"

"I am. Actually, I'm making hot cider punch. It's got pineapple juice, cranberry juice, apple juice, and an assortment of spices, including whole cinnamon sticks to make it nice and spicy. You wait and see. It's a tasty treat."

"Is it going to be an adult beverage?" he asked, sounding hopeful.

I laughed. "No. I'm making a child-friendly version for the party. You can add what you want later."

Maggie, my Bluetick hound, sat near my feet, looking up at me hopefully as I added ingredients to the crockpot. I reached a hand out and scratched her head.

Tonight was the annual fall party at the Sparrow Mountain Lodge. The lodge was owned by a local family and had two dozen cabins in the woods near the Snake River that could be rented by the night or week. The lodge itself had a large dining room, a recreation hall, and rooms that could be rented for parties or receptions. The fall party was held every October, and the price of admission was a dish to share with everyone and twenty dollars. The owners of the lodge provided the main dish, usually a roasted pig or other meat, and the money donated went to a local homeless shelter. I looked forward to it every year, and it would be more fun this year with someone to bring with me to snuggle with. Cade and I hadn't been dating long, but we were serious.

"So, what all are we going to do at this party? Is it adults only?" he asked, leaning on the kitchen counter. His chocolate-brown hair was neatly parted on the side, and he wore jeans and a red T-shirt.

"It's more of a family kind of get-together. There's a great big bonfire where we'll roast marshmallows, eat an assortment of yummy food, and all hang out and ooh and ah over the beautiful weather."

"Sounds like fun," he said. "Why aren't you making anything else?" He glanced around the kitchen.

"I made pumpkin bread and cranberry bread. I've been waiting all year to make these yummy fall treats," I said as I sprinkled some whole cloves into the punch. "You know me—I couldn't just make one dish."

"But it's not a Halloween party? I don't need a costume?" he asked.

I looked at him and grinned. "Did you want to wear a costume? Is that disappointment I hear in your voice?"

He chuckled. "No. Not even a tiny bit of disappointment. I was afraid I'd have to dress up as a mummy or Dracula."

"Never fear. The community center has a costume party on October 29th. Of course, the majority of the partygoers will be under twelve, but don't let that stop you from dressing up like a mummy and attending. You'll fit right in."

He chuckled. "I'll skip it. So when are we going to work on these floors?" he asked, looking at the chipped linoleum flooring in the kitchen. I had recently moved into a cute little cottage that still had a lot of original vintage touches. I wanted to update some of them, but keep the majority as is. The kitchen had cute scalloped-cut cupboards that had been popular in the forties. Of course, I was in love with the kitchen.

"I was thinking about that. I'm wondering if I can find some vintage reproduction linoleum online. If not, I think I'll try some tile. The linoleum in here has got to go. The chips and tears are too much to deal with. Oh, and I'm going to try to find some vintage wallpaper too."

"Wallpaper?"

"Yup. I want to make this kitchen look as authentic as possible, and without wallpaper, it won't look complete."

"The hardwood floors in the living room will have to be sanded and stained," he said, walking to the kitchen doorway and looking at the living room floor. "I think we can rent a floor sander down at the hardware store."

"That's a lot of work," I said, putting the lid back on the crockpot. I went to stand beside him.

"It is. But it's expensive to have a professional do the work," he said. "Besides, I'm handy. Kind of."

"I bet you can do anything you put your mind to. I love that you're handy with tools," I said, putting my arm around his waist. "I don't know what I'd do if I had to do it all on my own."

"I don't mind doing the work," he said and kissed me. Then he pulled back and looked at me.

"That's a serious look. What's up?" I asked.

"That ex-husband of yours. Is he gone?"

I eyed him. "He's gone. He had a doctor's appointment in New York. As much as I hate that he isn't well, I think he's staying in New York and I'm glad of that," I said. I was surprised that Cade was bothered about my ex-husband showing up in town. He was normally a laid-back person, but Cade had been asking about my ex-husband ever since he arrived in Sparrow a couple of months earlier. We had had a nasty divorce, and I had never wanted to see him again. But then he had suddenly shown up and said he wanted to apologize and to tell me he was dying.

"Good," he said and walked into the living room. "At least we've got the painting done in here." Cade was good at changing the subject.

I frowned. "You don't have to worry about him," I said, joining him in the living room.

"I'm not worried. I think we can get the floors done in here before Christmas," he said, changing the subject back. "We can work on the other rooms later. That way it will look nice in time for Christmas."

"I would love that," I said.

"Where are you going to put the Christmas tree?" he asked, turning toward me.

"Cade Starkey, are you sentimental about Christmas?" I asked, eyeing him.

He smiled with embarrassment. "Not me."

"I think you are. I love Christmas too. It reminds me of everything good about my childhood. Things haven't been the same since my dad died when I was nineteen, and Christmas brings back great family memories."

He nodded. "My mom died when I was sixteen. I hated Christmas for a long time because of the memories it brings back, but I'm looking forward to it this year."

I inhaled deeply. Cade glossed over a lot of things when we talked; his mother's death was one of them. It broke my heart that Christmas had been difficult for him in the past, but it made me happy that he was looking forward to it this year.

I went to him and put my arms around his waist again. "I was thinking about putting the tree right near the front window. That way the lights can be seen from the outside," I said. "And maybe we can put some lights up on the outside of the house. You don't mind ladders, do you?"

"They aren't my favorite, but I can do that," he said, leaning over and kissing the top of my head.

The doorbell rang before I could say anything else.

"I wonder who that could be?" I said and went to the door. I opened it and found my new neighbor standing on the doorstep. "Hello, Ida," I said.

"Hello, Rainey," she said with a smile. "I brought over some pumpkin spice cookies I made. I topped them with buttercream frosting." She held out a plastic Halloween-decorated plate with big cookies that were covered in clear plastic wrap.

"These look delicious," I said. "Thank you so much!" They did look delicious. They were drop cookies that were liberally frosted with buttercream frosting. I could smell the spices through the plastic wrap, and the aroma made my mouth water.

"I put walnuts and raisins in them. I hope you like walnuts and raisins," she said, smiling impishly. "My husband can't stand them, but I add them just to aggravate him."

I chuckled. "I love walnuts and raisins," I assured her. "I'm so glad you brought them by. I know Cade and I will enjoy them."

At the mention of his name, Cade came to the door, and I introduced them.

Ida looked him up and down and gave me a knowing smile. "I'm pleased to meet you," she said to him. "I'm so glad Rainey moved in here. It's been wonderful having her in the neighborhood."

Cade chuckled. "She does brighten up a place, doesn't she?"

Ida nodded. "That she does."

I felt my cheeks go pink. "It's sweet of you to bring the cookies by, Ida."

"It's my pleasure, dear. Well, I should get going. Burt will be wondering where I got off to. You kids enjoy," she said and turned and headed next door.

"Don't keep those to yourself," Cade said as I closed the door.

"I might keep them to myself. They smell wonderful," I said and unwrapped the edge of the plastic wrap so I could wiggle a cookie out. I handed it to Cade and got another for myself. I took a bite and groaned. They were soft and moist and the spices were exactly right.

"Wow, these are good. You've got competition," Cade said, putting the rest of the cookie into his mouth and reaching for another.

"I'd be offended by that, but I can't be. These are awesome," I said. "It's like a fall explosion in my mouth."

I was writing a cookbook with Americana-themed recipes and I wondered if I should ask Ida for the recipe for these cookies. I could give her credit when I published the book. I had a similar recipe, but I thought hers might be better.

Maggie bumped me with her nose and whined for a cookie. "I'll get you one of your cookies, Maggie," I said.

"These are great. I need some milk," he said and headed to the kitchen.

I followed after him. "We better not eat too many. There's going to be some great food at the party tonight. I'll snitch some of these in the middle of the night, though. I'm sure of it." I got one of Maggie's cookies from a jar I kept on the counter and gave it to her. She made it disappear instantly.

"Okay. But I might need to take some home with me," he said, pouring a glass of milk.

"I'll let you. Otherwise, I really will eat way too many of them."

I couldn't wait for the party. It was going to be a lot of fun, and it made the fall season all the more perfect.

IF YOU'D LIKE UPDATES on the newest books I'm writing, follow me on Amazon and Facebook:

https://www.facebook.com/
Kathleen-Suzette-Kate-Bell-authors-759206390932120/

https://www.amazon.com/Kathleen-Suzette/e/B07B7D2S4W/
ref=dp_byline_cont_pop_ebooks_1

Made in United States
Cleveland, OH
29 December 2024